FROM AMIGOS TO FRIENDS

by Pelayo "Pete" Garcia

PIÑATA BOOKS

PIÑATA BOOKS
HOUSTON, TEXAS
1997

This volume is made possible through grants from the National Endowment for the Arts (a federal agency), Andrew W. Mellon Foundation, the Lila Wallace-Reader's Digest Fund and the City of Houston through The Cultural Arts Council of Houston, Harris County.

Piñata Books are full of surprises!

Piñata Books
A Division of Arte Público Press
University of Houston
Houston, Texas 77204-2090

Cover illustration and design by Giovanni Mora

The paper used in this publication meets the requirements of the American National Standard for Permanence of Paper for Printed Library Materials Z39.48-1984.

FROM
AMIGOS
TO
FRIENDS

PROLOGUE

I was finally alone in my living room. I looked at my watch and couldn't believe how late it was. Tomorrow is a very special day, I thought. I should've gone to bed hours ago.

I cursed my next-door neighbors for staying so late. They kept on drinking even after everyone else had left our New Year's Eve party hours before. They didn't even flinch when my wife said good night in her pajamas and went to bed. Instead, they kept on telling bad jokes.

In the kitchen, I took twelve grapes out of the refrigerator and ate eleven of them as I made my New Year's wishes. I knew it wouldn't work, considering midnight had long passed and because for many years I had refused to eat the required twelfth grape. It was a silly superstition, but I wasn't taking any chances.

I went into my eleven-year-old son's room to kiss him good night and found on the nightstand next to his bed an empty bowl with a few grape seeds and one grape left untouched.

I kissed his cheek and sat on a chair next to the bed. He's a good kid, down to avoiding the twelfth grape just like his Dad, I thought, closing my eyes to think back.

CHAPTER I

Sitting on his bed in the dark, David Oviedo made his eleventh wish and ate the eleventh grape. One to go.

"Eat these twelve grapes tonight at the stroke of midnight," David's father had told him earlier that night. "It's an old Cuban New Year's tradition. You'll be granted twelve wishes and twelve months of good luck during the coming year of 1959."

I doubt this will work, he thought, picking up the twelfth grape.

He suddenly noticed both hands of his watch resting on the number twelve. He would turn twelve in twelve days. Oh, my God! He decided to skip the twelfth grape and quickly made the sign of the cross just in case so many twelves were a bad omen. In record time, he made more signs of the cross. It was only a precaution, but well worth the effort.

Rapid gunfire suddenly shattered the serenity of the night, and the flash from fireworks lit the bedroom.

David jumped out of bed and ran to his parents' bathroom. He flipped the light switch. Eight seconds! That was close, he thought. His big brown eyes darted suspiciously around the spacious, marble bathroom. Eight seconds of exposure in the darkness, away from the safety of his bed, was okay if he wore Roy Rogers pajamas. He allowed ten seconds with Batman and a full twelve with his Superman pajamas.

David wetted the shaving brush in the sink and whipped up the shaving soap dish into a lather. He opened his father's straightedge razor and instantly had second thoughts. He considered using the dull edge, but concluded that Carlos or Luis would question him, and then he'd be laughed out of town. So he practiced with the dull edge until he became confident.

His plan had jelled right after his mother and father had left with Carlos' parents to celebrate New Year's Eve at Tropicana, the fanciest nightclub in Havana. David had previously asked his parents to allow him to spend the night with Carlos and Luis, but he was turned down without a moment of consideration. As a result, the boys had agreed to do something adult-like on their own on New Year's Eve. The next day they would surprise and impress each other with their individual accomplishment.

With a shaky hand, David now placed the sharp edge to his sideburn and carefully pressed down against his skin. He was fully done with the right side of his face when he became overconfident and cut himself. To his horror, blood trickled down his face. I'm bleeding. What do I do? What would my father do? He ripped a yard of toilet paper off the wall-mounted dispenser and pressed the wad of paper against the scratch, his hand shaking even more now. Praying for his life, he removed the toilet paper from the wound. The bleeding seemed to have stopped. Oh no! I'm still bleeding. The blood resumed trickling down his face. What if I can't stop it? How much blood can I spare until I pass out and they find me dead in a pool of blood? "HELP!" The word escaped out of his mouth. "HELP!"

Reaching the point when he decided that one more drop would make survival beyond hope, David grabbed his weekly allowance and headed for the maid's room, turning on every light in his path. He accepted having to pay María five pesos: one for stopping the bleeding and four for keeping her mouth shut. If there was one thing his father had taught him, it was to take responsibility for his actions.

From Amigos to Friends

Two short blocks down the street, lying in bed smoking a cigarette, chewing gum, and viewing one of his father's magazines full of naked women, Carlos Fernández daydreamed about how it would feel to squeeze the incredibly big melons on the bleached blonde on the page in front of him. On the nightstand, a portable shortwave radio his parents had reluctantly given him two weeks ago for his twelfth birthday was tuned to WFUN, Miami's top rock-and-roll station.

Carlos snapped to attention when Elvis began singing "You Ain't Nothin' But a Hound Dog." He jumped out of bed in his white Jockey shorts and in front of a full-length mirror on the bathroom door, rolled his skinny hips to the pulsating music. His blond hair was combed like Elvis' and he stared with pride into green eyes that matched his idol's. The song over, he returned to bed, pulled on the cigarette, and had a sudden coughing fit. He hoped that Luis was right and that he would finally get the hang of it before he died coughing.

He loved his shortwave radio. It gave him access to rock-and-roll at any hour of the day, instead of the boring Latin music played by local Cuban stations. His record collection had helped him survive in the past, but it took too long, sometimes a whole week, for new top-ten 45s to reach the record stores in Miramar, the affluent coastal suburb of Havana where he lived. The memory of his parents handing him a chemistry set with a microscope for his birthday still upset him. It had then taken him two weeks of fits and expert manipulation to get what he wanted, but it had been well worth the effort, he thought as he affectionately patted the radio.

Carlos heard a car pull into the driveway. He went outside on his balcony and was caught off guard by his parents returning early. He bolted back inside. In the middle of the room, he hesitated. Should he get rid of the cigarette or turn off the radio first? The light wasn't a give away, since he slept with it on. Nothing to be proud of, but he was addicted to it. Deciding that the radio was easier to explain, he flushed the cigarette down the toilet. Back next to his bed, he turned off the radio and quickly jumped in bed as the front door shut. He felt the magazine against his back and panicked.

Three choices flashed through his mind. Blame his sister. No, that would not work this time. Stay in bed and put the magazine back in its place tomorrow. That would only work if his father was tired. Or run! He slid and fell, making the turn out of his bedroom into the hallway. Back on his feet, he accelerated past the upstairs phone nook and, at full speed, ran into his father's closet. On the return leg, Carlos heard them coming up the stairs. He raced into his bedroom, leaped into bed, and threw the sheets over his shoulders.

❦

Several blocks beyond where the expensive homes in Miramar ended, in a one-room apartment, on the second floor of a run-down building over a noisy twenty-four-hour coffee shop in front of an always-crowded bus stop at the congested intersection of 110th Street and 10th Avenue, Luis Rodríguez slowly lowered his unruly mop of black hair until it rested on his pillow.

The room again began to move as if pivoting on his nose. Closing his eyes only accelerated the spinning. Opening them seemed momentarily to slow the room down, but then the ceiling took off like a 78 RPM record. He raised up on his elbows, and the spinning slowed down to where there was hope he wouldn't start the New Year barfing all over himself.

He cautiously turned on his side, closed his eyes and very, very slowly lowered himself onto his right shoulder. His cheek touched the pillow. His entire body was soaked in cold perspiration. His feet felt as if covered with ice. His stomach churned like a washing machine. His mouth was dry and tasted like the time when he had vomited after eating four cream cheese and guava paste sandwiches.

For a moment, the room kept still. He was sure it was because he was squeezing his eyes shut as hard as he could.

Then, sensing the onset of a suspicious motion, he finally broke down. "Please, God. Help me! Make the room stop spinning."

He was certain that he was dying. He had to snap out of it. He was thankful he had only taken a few swallows from his father's bottle of Bacardi rum. One more gulp and I would be dead, he suspected. I wonder if Papi would cry.

The room took off again. This time Luis jumped out of bed, scared out of his mind that he might die.

Standing straight up in the middle of the room, he heard his parents' voices outside in the hallway.

"Mami! Papi!" Luis heard his older sister yell from the hallway. "Luis is inside getting drunk!"

"That's it," Luis said between shudders of fear. "First thing tomorrow morning, I'll kill her!"

He heard rapid footsteps approaching.

Snatching the bottle of rum off the floor, he started to run, but slipped and fell on a pile of his mother's sewing. On his knees, he then sped into the bathroom, where he flung the bottle out the window.

Then, with a huge heave, he threw up all over the bare concrete floor.

"LUISITO!"

"LUISITO!"

CHAPTER II

The next morning, Carlos was awakened by a blaring radio newscast pounding through the wall separating him from his sister's room. Suddenly remembering that she did not have a radio, Carlos opened his eyes and found his shortwave radio missing. He ran to her bedroom. It was locked. He banged on the door.

No answer. Carlos only heard the radio announcer bark in rapid Cuban-Spanish, "General Fulgencio Batista—three-time President of the Cuban Republic, once by a military coup, and twice elected, but not by fair elections, of course—has in the middle of the night fled the island in a plane full of family members, cronies and suitcases stuffed with millions of U.S. dollars... every cent extorted during years of coercion, graft, bribery, blackmail and all other known corrupt methods, including several invented under his brutal dictatorship. Down with Batista! ¡*Viva* Fidel! ¡*Viva* the Revolution!"

Carlos pounded on his sister's door while Rocky, his two-hundred-pound German shepherd began barking ferociously.

The radio commentator proceeded to recall Fidel Castro's invasion a few years back; a seven-day voyage from Mexico in a run-down fishing boat that had transported Fidel with eighty-one guerrillas back to Cuba. Sixty of Fidel's men were killed and another fifteen were arrested. Fidel, his brother Raúl, Argentine intellectual Che Guevara and four others had narrowly escaped into the bush.

13

Carlos tried to knock the door down. He nearly fractured his shoulder and ended up on the floor howling in pain. Rocky howled at the door.

The radio announcer then recapped how dictator Batista's forty-thousand troops, fully equipped with the best U.S. military hardware that American foreign aid could buy, were regularly trounced by Fidel's band of less than one thousand poorly armed revolutionaries.

Disgusted with his sister, Carlos marched into his parents' bedroom and demanded that they immediately break her door down and rescue his radio.

All he got was his father's sarcasm and more of the same newscast: "...With two hundred million dollars, a villa on his own private island off the coast of Spain, and only a few days from his sixtieth birthday, Batista just decided it was time to retire."

Carlos secretly vowed to make his parents miserable until they retrieved his shortwave radio. Then, he would be able to tune in to WFUN in Miami and avoid the interminable political blah, blah, blah he knew would follow for days on end.

In the Oviedo's dining room, David stuffed himself with buttered toast and orange marmalade while his parents listened intently to the same radio newscast.

David protested in vain when his father, alarmed with the news on the radio, prohibited David from leaving the house. Mr. Oviedo then pointed out how the country had prospered during Batista's reign. His father cited statistics and details about the economy.

David shook his head, puzzled at how his father knew so much about so many different subjects, and yet he did not know Mickey Mantle's career batting average.

The doorbell rang and David ran to answer the front door, hoping to find Carlos and Luis. Instead, Carlos' father unexpectedly rushed inside the house. His fair skin was flushed and his bald head was covered with perspiration.

"The seamstress, Luis' mother, is at my house having an attack," he announced, out of breath. "She needs a doctor!"

Dr. Oviedo quickly left the room.

Mr. Fernández collapsed on his neighbor's couch. "When her husband heard that Batista fled, he took a bus in the middle of the night to CMQ and led the mob that took over the TV station in the name of the Revolution!"

"That's crazy," Mr. Oviedo said. "Isn't he some kind of night watchman?"

"What do you expect? Why do you think it's called a revolution? Now that it's safe, a lot of frustrated nobodies are going to be more revolutionary than Fidel. You'll see."

"I don't have any good feelings about Castro," Mr. Oviedo said.

"What are you saying? That he's a Communist? Nonsense. That was just part of Batista's propaganda to discredit the Revolution," Mr. Fernández said.

David cringed when Mr. Fernández ceremoniously took a foot-long Partagas cigar from the breast pocket of his impeccably pressed white linen suit and bit off the tip. David had seen it done before.

"How can he be a Communist?" Mr. Fernández continued. "He studied at the same exclusive private Catholic school you attended." He expertly sucked on the end of the cigar until it was perfectly wet.

"That only proves my point. Twelve years under those priests and you either come out an atheist or a retired Catholic like me. So why not a Communist?"

"Look, even if he's a Communist, do you think the Americans are going to allow a Communist country ninety miles from the United States?" Mr. Fernández asked, savoring the deep tobacco aroma from his expensive cigar.

"I guess you're right. We have nothing to worry about."

Mr. Fernández lit the cigar, inhaled and slowly blew a thick, dark cloud over them. David remembered throwing up at this very moment in the ritual, the day Luis had convinced him and Carlos to smoke one of Mr. Fernández's cigars.

Dr. Oviedo rushed out of the house with her black medical bag in hand. David left with his mother, taking advantage of the opportunity to get out of the house. They hurried down a street lined with royal palms and elegant homes in route to Carlos' house.

When they arrived in front of Carlos' two-story, white stucco Spanish mansion, David heard his friend's bird call coming from the mango tree on the side of the house. David fell behind as his mother rushed up the steps of the front porch. He spotted Carlos up a tree, munching on a golden mango and spying through a window into his own living room. David quickly climbed the tree and perched himself on a branch near Carlos. Through the open window he saw Mrs. Rodríguez, Luis' mother, collapsed on an enormous living room couch with her face buried in her hands and sobbing loudly.

There was a knock on the front door and with a bewildered look on her face, a black maid in white uniform led Dr. Oviedo into the room. David's mother stepped over Rocky who was asleep by the front door, and rushed to her patient's side.

David picked a ripe mango dangling over his head and settled in for the show.

"I can't get her to calm down," Mrs. Fernández, who was Carlos' mother, said. "She won't even have a cup of coffee."

"I'll have some," Doctor Oviedo said, while taking Mrs. Rodríguez's pulse with one hand and propping an eyelid open with the other. She inspected each eye in great detail while Mrs. Rodríguez wailed.

"Is she having a nervous breakdown?" Mrs. Fernández asked. The maid arrived with an Art Nouveau porcelain coffee set on a matching tray.

"I should've been born in the United States," Dr. Oviedo shouted over the seamstress', wails and poured herself a cup of coffee. "I can't stand these Latin dramas. All she needs is some rest."

Carlos and David nodded in agreement. They too preferred rock-and-roll and major league baseball to Latin drama.

"Sugar?" Mrs. Fernández offered.

"No, thank you. I'm trying to keep my weight under control while I'm pregnant," David's mother said.

David almost fell out of the tree. Pregnant? Had he heard his mother correctly? Carlos, of course, immediately started making fun of him.

"Have you already told David that he's going to have a little brother or sister?"

"No, I don't have the heart. Let him be an only child for a little while longer."

There was no doubt now—his life was ruined forever, David concluded. Carlos did not stop laughing until David hit him in the head with the half-eaten mango.

"We spoil our boys way too much," David's mother said.

Luis' mother wailed.

"I can't help it," Carlos' mother said. "Carlitos deserves to be spoiled. He's so sweet, and smart, and beautiful." Picking up the coffee pot, she offered Dr. Oviedo a refill.

"Just a splash, please."

"I hope this revolution doesn't spoil my trip to Miami," Mrs. Fernández said, pouring the coffee.

"It won't last. We've had twenty-one presidents since the Americans helped us gain our independence from Spain fifty-seven years ago."

"That many?"

"What are you going to shop for in Miami this time?"

"The usual. Clothes, records for my little angel, odds and ends. Probably a new car."

"But your Cadillac is brand new."

"Oh no, it's two years old," Mrs. Fernández said.

Mrs. Rodríguez wailed, "He's finally gone mad! I've lost him to the Revolution!"

"She arrived to do some embroidery for me and mentioned something about a problem with her son Luis when she and her husband got home last night," Mrs. Fernández explained to Dr. Oviedo.

Carlos laughed and signaled to David that Luis had been hitting the bottle. David shook his head disapprovingly.

"She then told me about her husband taking over the TV station in the name of Fidel and the Revolution, and then she broke down and became hysterical," Mrs. Fernández said.

"Does he work there?"

"He does now."

"Anarchy!"

"You know men. Never satisfied with what they have."

"We women should run the country," Dr. Oviedo said.

"No, thanks. More coffee?"

Mrs. Rodríguez now gasped through her sobs, "He's finally gone mad! I've lost him to the Revolution!"

That afternoon, in an empty lot next to his house, David slid at full speed onto an old newspaper serving as second base. Carlos' throw sailed over David's ankle to lodge in Luis' glove, which slapped David's knee.

"You're out!" Carlos and Luis yelled simultaneously.

"I'm safe!" David argued, dusting off his new pants.

Carlos took off toward his friends, the catcher's mask bouncing on top of his head, the shin guards flapping around his skinny legs.

With arms crossed, David firmly stood his ground on top of the old newspaper. "I was safe!" he said. "I won."

"Get off that base! You're out!" Carlos said, throwing the mask and catcher's mitt on the ground.

Luis stood behind David and started laughing.

David raised his skinny fists. "Come on, you little turd. Come and get what you deserve."

Carlos put up his even skinnier arms. "You're the turd... a big turd," Carlos said and pushed him. David stumbled backward, but kept one foot on the old newspaper.

They shoved each other back and forth, while Luis laughed.

David felt the seat of his brand new shorts and to his horror felt a huge rip. He knew he'd catch hell from his mother, but for now he put all fears on the back burner. He was dealing with a more crucial matter: his manhood was on the line.

David shoved Luis hard to the ground, but Carlos began chanting insults at David's funny underwear as soon as Luis stopped.

What rotten luck, David thought, now chasing the chanting Carlos around the lot. My pants would have to rip the day I'm wearing the stupid boxer shorts covered with little red teddy bears. Never again. They're going in the trash the minute I get home. Only white Jockey shorts from now on, he vowed. He leapt on Carlos' back, and they both fell hard on the ground. Carlos, gasping for air, kept taunting David who was now choking him to death.

Luis heard it first. It was a mob advancing down the street, yelling revolutionary slogans: "Down with the government! Death to Batista! Fidel! Fidel! Fidel!"

The boys rushed to the corner and joined the crowd as it headed in the direction of Carlos' house. They were about thirty in number, mostly angry young men, the type that David's father accused of always complaining about the lack of opportunities. "There are plenty of jobs if one is willing to work hard. If they worked as hard as they complained, they would be rich. They want everything now. Don't they know change takes time? They'd rather sit on the floor than spend time building a chair!"

At first, the boys tailed the mob close enough not to miss anything, but far enough away to avoid trouble if their parents spotted them. David covered the rip in his shorts with the baseball glove.

The rhythmic yelling, the pounding of feet against the pavement, the strength of their developed muscles, the tension on their faces, the anger in their eyes mesmerized and lured the boys farther down the street. Carlos tensed as they neared his house.

The leader, a tall, dark man, suddenly searched the ground and found a baseball-size rock. Fueled by the anger emanating from his eyes, his muscular arm heaved the stone over the ten-foot concrete wall circling senator Del Valle's mansion. A second-story window shattered into a thousand pieces.

The mob went wild. Rocks started flying. More windows exploded. Some of the men yelled obscenities, insults. Others climbed the fence. One man pissed on the wall as others laughed out of control. David panicked and dropped to the ground, knowing that guards armed with machine guns constantly guarded the property. Carlos and Luis did the same, but nothing happened. They realized the place was abandoned, unprotected.

The leader appeared inside the front gate. He flung the steel doors wide open. The mob stood in front of the open gate screaming, laughing, but hesitant to go inside the property. One of the men who had scaled the wall came out through the gate with a huge grin on his face, a television set under one arm and a radio under the other.

The mob stormed the gate.

"They're going to kill Roberto and his family," David gasped.

"They're in Miami," Carlos said. "They're spending the holidays there."

"Where are the guards?" David asked.

"You're so stupid," Luis said. "Don't you know Batista left Cuba last night?"

"It doesn't matter what that mob does," Carlos said, pointing at the looters. "Now Roberto and his family won't be back. They'll stay in the United States."

"I'm going to live in the United States when I grow up," David said. "I'm going to play in the major leagues."

"I'm getting out of here too," Carlos said. "I'm going to start a rock-and-roll band in New York."

"You're both full of shit," Luis said. "Your mamas won't even let you cross the street by yourselves... even after you grow up."

Carlos held Luis down while David punched Luis' arm. The attack on Luis was interrupted when they saw a man come out from behind the wall, pushing a baby carriage stuffed full of food.

"Was Roberto's father part of Batista's team?" David asked.

"Why do you think they had guards with machine guns, dummy?" Luis said. "His father was a senator."

"My father told me Roberto's father was a gangster. My mother warned me never to go in his house," David said.

"What a great combination," Luis said, "a gangster and a senator at the same time."

"I knew him really well," Carlos said.

"You knew the father? The gangster?" David asked.

"No, Roberto."

"He never came outside the wall," Luis said. "Liar."

Two men, drenched in sweat, came out through the gate carrying a refrigerator as one would carry a man on a stretcher.

"Have you ever been inside the wall?" David asked in awe.

"I have," Carlos said proudly.

A barefoot man bent over at the waist stumbled outside the gate with a king-size mattress on his back.

"What's it like to hold one of the guard's machine guns?" Luis asked.

"We played catch," Carlos said.

"You threw a stupid baseball around," Luis said, "when you could've had a real machine gun! You're stupid."

"One of the guards was teaching us how to throw a slider."

"That's how you learned how?" David asked.

Three men came out through the gate carrying a sofa loaded with lamps, chairs, tables, pillows. A lamp fell off the couch and crashed onto the pavement. The sofa moved on.

"Those guards were killers," Luis said. "They wouldn't play baseball with two little mama's boys. Liar!"

"Luis!" David said, "shut up!"

"We used to play in his room. I've never seen so many games and toys in my life."

"What kind of stuff does he have?" Luis asked.

An old man on a brand new three-speed bicycle wove out the gate with a burlap sack flung over his shoulder. He hit the curb, flew over the handlebars and landed on his hands and knees as cans of food scattered all over the sidewalk.

"What kind of stuff does he have?" Luis asked again.

"You name it, he has it."

"And they're still behind those walls," Luis pointed out, grinning. "I want a machine gun!"

"He doesn't have any," Carlos said.

"No, stupid. I want one of the guard's machine guns," Luis said.

"Luis, you're crazy," David and Carlos said together.

A kid their age, wearing a man's tuxedo, came out through the gate hauling away a huge bundle of men's suits, "Fidel! Fidel! Fidel!" he chanted.

"Carlos, what do you want from behind those walls?" Luis asked.

"Nothing," he replied. "I wouldn't take anything from Roberto. He's my friend."

"Why not? You said it didn't matter what those people are doing," Luis said, pointing at the people coming in and out of the gate, sacking the mansion across the street. "Roberto isn't coming back."

Carlos kicked a rock and said, "David, what do you think? Luis is right. Roberto is not coming back."

"I'm not going in there," David said. "My father would kill me."

"If you two turds don't make up your minds," Luis said, "there won't be anything left worth taking."

Carlos and Luis looked at each other. "David," Carlos said, "in his bedroom there's a big collection of autographed baseballs. Major-league stuff."

"Come on, girls!" Luis said.

"Are you sure Roberto is not coming back?" David asked, wondering where he could hide the autographed baseballs so that his father would not find them.

"Positive!" Luis said.

"I didn't ask you, Luis."

"I'm sure," Carlos said with authority.

"It's still not right," David said, sitting down on the curb.

Carlos and Luis then crossed the street and reached the gate as a new, shiny black Cadillac packed with household goods was pulling out. The electric window on the driver's side slid down and the angry face of the leader of the mob appeared right in front of Carlos' face. "Hey, rich kid, get ready. Your houses are next!"

Pelayo "Pete" Garcia

The Cadillac burned rubber away from the gate, and the boys fled, each in the direction of his own home.

CHAPTER III

The first week under the Revolution was one big Latin party. The entire country readily obeyed Fidel when he ordered a seven-day general strike while he descended from the mountains and slowly, triumphantly paraded across the island all the way to Havana. For a whole week David witnessed on television a slow parade of open trucks and convertibles loaded down with an assortment of bearded, long-haired revolutionaries wielding their firearms in the air. They wore soiled, olive-green combat uniforms accessorized with rosaries around their necks and crucifixes nestled on their hairy chests.

Fidel's parade climaxed in Havana on January 8, when a corpulent and bearded Fidel, with a white dove resting on his left shoulder, delivered a mesmerizing four-hour speech in front of a crowd of a hundred thousand spectators. The remaining population of seven million watched the hypnotic speech on television. David's father insisted that the whole family endure the entire four hours, calling the speech historic, regardless of how time would eventually judge Castro.

Through February, Fidel's marathon television speeches preempted all other programs, from cartoons to winter league professional baseball. During one of those speeches, Fidel pointed out that the constitution needed to be modified to fully support the Revolution's needs, including the deletion of the right of citizens to private ownership and the creation of absolute government power to confiscate any and all privately owned property. Fidel accused anyone opposing the changes as "Counterrevolutionaries!" Fidel yelled, pumping his fists. "Anyone against constitutional reform is against the Revolution. They are greedy worms, only out to protect their self-interest at the expense of the people!" The crowd chanted back, "Fidel! Fidel! Fidel!" David heard his father predict that his architectural firm would be out of business within two months.

The next month, Dr. Oviedo gave birth. It turned out to be not as bad as David had expected. His mother survived, his father took him out of school early to go to the hospital, and "it" was not a sister. Except for the baby crying all the time and his parents' silly baby-talk, David's life basically remained the same as before.

A month after the birth, Mr. Oviedo picked up his son from school for the long lunch break and they drove to the barbershop. Neither one of them needed a haircut, but, why not, there was nothing else to do. As his father had predicted, all his clients had canceled the building projects Mr. Oviedo's firm had been designing and with no work he had been forced to let go of all twelve employees. Besides, the barber was a good listener and always told the funniest political jokes and newest gossip. David enjoyed talking baseball with the barber, because although he wore a funny looking pencil-thin mustache, he knew even more lifetime batting averages than David himself.

At the barbershop they found five businessmen sitting around waiting. All of them looked as if their hair had been cut that week. Assuming that the five haircuts could not possibly take long, David and his father sat down.

"You know the story of how Che Guevara got to become minister of the economy?" the barber asked the businessman sitting in the barber chair. The barber always spoke loud enough to entertain everyone in his shop. "One day in the mountains when Fidel asked a gathering of his top men if there was an economist in the group, Che raised his hand, mistakenly hearing Fidel ask if there was a Communist in the group. Che explained the misunderstanding by blaming it on his hearing loss from firing a bazooka at Batista's troops for three years straight in the..."

By the third haircut, David had finished every magazine in the barbershop. His father became more and more impatient by the minute. Making matters worse, the barber was not his usual funny self. Instead of his polished stand-up act loaded with sarcastic political jokes and juicy gossip, he was in a foul mood.

"So many of my regular clients are leaving Cuba, I'm either going to have to learn another occupation or move to Miami," the barber complained.

Mr. Oviedo suddenly became short of breath. David noticed that perspiration covered his father's forehead. The barber opened a straight razor and slowly sharpened the blade, back and forth, on a leather strap hanging behind the barber chair. When the barber tilted the man's head forward and pressed the cold, razor-sharp steel edge against the back of the client's neck, David's father started hyperventilating. He then bolted out of his chair and ran outside. David ran after his father and did not catch him until they reached their house, three blocks away. The '57 Dodge was left behind, parked in front of the barbershop.

Mr. Oviedo lay down in bed without taking off his shoes. He covered himself with a sheet up to his chin, while his wife took his pulse and patiently listened to her husband retell the incident. David hid behind the doorjamb, listening to every word.

"There's nothing physically wrong with you," she said, taking off her stethoscope. "But I'm making an appointment for you to see Dr. Blanco."

"Dr. Blanco?" he asked as if she had made a mistake.

"Yes, that's who I said."

"Isn't he a psychiatrist?"

"You're under a lot of stress..."

"I'm not crazy," he said firmly. "I won't go to a psychiatrist."

"You don't need to be crazy to see a psychiatrist," she said affectionately. "It's mental health that..."

"You think I'm going crazy, don't you?"

She kissed him and said, "You're not crazy. You're under a lot of stress. You'll like Dr. Blanco. He won't cut your hair, but he's a great listener."

"I don't want David to know that I'm going to see a psychiatrist," he said as his wife left his side to go take care of their sons. "I don't want him to think I'm crazy."

David then took three well-practiced leaps and belly-flopped on the bed next to his father. "Papi, are you sick?"

"No, just resting before lunch."

"Why did we run back from the barbershop?"

"It was fun, wasn't it?"

"Are you sure you're not sick?"

"I'm fine. Ask your mother if you want a second opinion."

"When am I going to get a three-speed bike?" David asked, staring at a big black hair sticking out of his father's ear.

"What's wrong with your bike?"

"It's only one speed. It's too slow." David hoped he would never start growing hair out of his ears.

"Are you racing with your bike again?" Mr. Oviedo asked, giving David a suspicious look.

From Amigos to Friends

The first bicycle accident had involved a head-on collision with a concrete wall when David's tricycle failed to make a sharp curve. David's four front teeth bit a hole through his tongue big enough to put a finger through. "We're lucky he didn't have more teeth," his mother had said to her husband. "If he had, he would have bitten his tongue off." David had drank so much of his own blood, he caught a rare disease that made his skin turn blue for twelve days.

"No, Papi, I'm not," David said, crossing all his fingers behind his back.

—————

During a speech in May, Fidel ordered the creation of an agrarian reform program. Heralded as the crown jewel of the Revolution, the reform allowed farmlands to be confiscated from their owners. The land now belonged to the Revolution. Cooperative farms were run by agents of the Revolution, not agricultural experts. Carlos heard his father predict that the country was headed toward food shortages and that the island was going to empty out from people escaping the hunger by taking to the sea toward the United States in anything they could find that floated.

Carlos sat on the private school bus, wondering what it would be like to get home for lunch one day and find nothing to eat. The school bus stopped in front of Carlos' house. With his uniform's shirttail dangling, his tie knot halfway down his chest and chocolate stains on his short khaki pants, Carlos jumped off the bus and ran inside through the front door. His older sister gingerly stepped down from the bus and slowly reached the front porch. Alicia's uniform was impeccably pressed, befitting her stature as senior class president of the exclusive co-ed school she and Carlos attended. She was halfway through the door when Carlos leaped from behind it. She screamed and her books flew up in the air. She kept on screaming until her mother appeared, but Carlos had already fled.

Carlos found refuge inside his father's walk-in closet. He kept quiet, trying not to laugh. He was so excited that he had to hold on to his penis to prevent wetting his pants. He heard his mother and sister yelling his name, searching for him throughout the house. Since his parents' French-antiques-furnished bedroom was absolutely off-limits, he felt confident that they would not look for him there. They might check inside the bedroom, but would never search his father's closet, since Mr. Fernández prohibited everyone, including his wife, from entering his closet. Carlos felt safe, knowing his father would not be home for lunch for another half-hour.

"What's all this screaming about?" Mr. Fernández yelled as he slammed the front door shut.

Carlos froze.

Mr. Fernández quickly went up the stairs, his daughter and wife trailing closely behind.

"Papi, you have to punish Carlos. He's trying to give me a heart attack!"

"Now, now," Mrs. Fernández said, defending her son. "He was just playing."

"Mami, you're always taking his side," Alicia complained.

Still inside the closet, Carlos heard them approaching and decided that by then it was too late to make a run for it. The closet was the best place to hide and not be found. But if his father caught him in his closet, Carlos feared the worst. He imagined being grounded until he got married. Worse yet, his father would throw away his radio, hi-fi record player and records. Or maybe just torture him until a slow death ended his pain.

"Papi, spank him and teach him a lesson."

"Young lady!" Mrs. Fernández said, appalled. "We don't believe in violence in this house."

From Amigos to Friends

Mr. Fernández reached the bedroom door, faced his daughter and wife and shouted, "Why don't you both shut up!" He stepped into his bedroom and slammed the door in their faces.

Carlos held on to his penis—this time out of terror instead of excitement. He heard his father's heavy footsteps approaching the closet. He closed his eyes and held his breath.

"You are so rude," Carlos heard his mother say, entering the room and shutting the door behind her. "You constantly hurt her feelings. I'm used to it, but she's just a girl."

In the dark, Carlos sensed a heavy hand turn the closet's door handle.

"Did you listen to a word I said?" his mother demanded to know.

"If you'd spend less time shopping and more time controlling the kids, we'd have fewer problems."

"I see," she said. "It's all my fault."

"I come home early for a little peace and quiet, and I find a madhouse."

"The kids were just playing. You should be thankful that they are healthy and active," she said.

"Carlos is out of control, and Alicia acts like a princess."

Carlos swallowed hard.

"If you'd spend more time with them," his mother fired back, "they might improve."

"You're the mother. It's your responsibility."

"Carlos needs more time with you," she said.

Carlos nodded, his forehead covered with perspiration.

"I don't have the time," he said. "I have a business to run."

Carlos heard his mother storm out of the room, and then the bedroom door slammed shut. He predicted that the end was near. In his mind's eye, he followed his father to the closet. Finding him on his knees pleading for mercy, his father then pulled a revolver from a secret, hidden compartment. The cold, round barrel pressed against the back of Carlos' neck. He pleaded for another chance to redeem himself. He promised to go to church every Sunday, never lie again, be nice to his sister and her friends, give Rocky a bath once a week, never talk back, get straight A's in school, keep his room clean, eat codfish, stop playing with himself, never smoke a cigarette again... The gun went off. The bullet pierced his spine.

Hearing his father dialing the phone, Carlos suddenly came out of his imaginary tragedy.

"Linda?"

Carlos' mind raced through its memory file, but did not register any Linda.

"I'm coming over right after lunch and I'm going to have you for dessert," his father said.

Carlos moved next to the closet door to hear better. He closed one eye and peeked through the keyhole. His father lay on the bed with his head propped up on a pillow, a big grin on his face.

"You really want me to tell you on the phone what I'm going to do to you this afternoon?"

Carlos felt his head throbbing.

"I'm going to rip off your clothes with my teeth and then I'm going to lick you from head to toe until you scream."

Carlos decided his father was playing a game with a friend and smiled.

"After I've ripped off your clothes and licked you, I'm going to use your nylons to tie you to the bed so I can ravish you."

Carlos got an erection.

"No, you won't be able to scream because I'll stuff my underwear in your mouth."

Carlos started touching himself.

"No, of course I've never done that to my wife," he said with disgust.

Carlos stopped touching himself.

From Amigos to Friends

"She's too old and fat," he said and broke out laughing.

Carlos' erection disappeared.

"You're the only one I love."

Carlos fell away from the door.

"I'll be there in an hour, but first I have to do my duty here."

Carlos reached for his father's favorite tie and ripped it apart.

"Yes, one day you won't be alone at lunch time. But you have to be patient."

Carlos covered his ears with his hands and pressed as hard as he could.

"I'll see you in bed in an hour." His father hung up the phone and left the bedroom.

⚊⚊⚊

Ignoring his father and his sister sitting at the dining room table waiting for lunch to be served, Carlos moved past them and went into the kitchen.

The maid was busy emptying a pot into a serving dish, while his mother checked to make sure that the taste was up to her standards. Carlos reached his mother, wrapped his arms around her ample waist and buried his face in her dress.

"Mami, I think you're beautiful."

His mother hugged and kissed him. "Carlitos, Carlitos, you can be so sweet when you want to be," Mrs. Fernández said and held him close to her. "Go on, go sit down. We're eating in a minute."

Carlos again buried his face in her dress. "I don't want lunch. I want to go to my room," he mumbled.

"Are you sick?" she asked, feeling his forehead.

He shook his head. "I'm not hungry," he mumbled.

"Come on, my little prince," she said, leading him by the hand into the dining room. "If you eat all your lunch, I'll give you a bowl of chocolate ice cream for dessert."

Carlos and his mother took their places at the table.

"Papi, Carlos was sent to the principal's office this morning," Alicia announced. "Weren't you, Carlos?"

Everyone looked at Carlos, who stared into emptiness.

"Carlitos," Mrs. Fernández said, alarmed. "Why were you sent to the principal's office?"

Carlos kept silent. Under the table, he petted his dog Rocky.

"He was caught pinching Teresita Gómez's behind at recess," Alicia said, savoring the moment. "That's why."

Mr. Fernández smiled.

"I'm sure it was all a misunderstanding," Mrs. Fernández said, relieved. "Let's eat the soup before it gets cold. Carlitos, eat your soup so you can have some ice cream for dessert."

Carlos' sister shook her head. "Papi, I'm going to graduate first in my class," Alicia announced.

"Sweetheart, that's great news. We're so proud of you," Mrs. Fernández said, trying to get her husband to join her in praising his daughter.

"Papi," Alicia said, "If I graduate first in my class, can we spend an extra week in Miami this summer?"

The maid came into the dining room and collected three empty soup plates. Mrs. Fernández nodded, signaling the maid to take away Carlos' full soup plate and serve the garlic chicken with french fries.

"No! We're not going to Miami," he casually said, and bit into the chicken leg.

Daughter and mother stared at each other. She then looked at her son, expecting him to start having a fit, but instead he sat quietly while he surreptitiously fed Rocky pieces of chicken under the table.

"We're not?" Mrs. Fernández asked, breaking a long period of silence.

"No!"

From Amigos to Friends

"Why not?" Carlos' sister demanded to know from her father.

"I'll tell you why, little princess," Mr. Fernández began, his voice rising in volume with every word. "We don't have the money. My dealership hasn't sold a Pontiac in months. First of all, I'm not getting any more cars from Detroit and, second, nobody is buying new cars!" His last words were screamed at his daughter.

Alicia ran out of the room crying. Mrs. Fernández followed her daughter, trying to console her.

Carlos was left alone with his father. He looked up from his plate and stared at his father who was rushing to finish lunch.

"Papi, I have the afternoon off from school."

His father nodded and continued to eat the last few pieces of meat on his chicken leg.

"If things are slow at the dealership, why don't you stay home this afternoon and teach me to throw a knuckle ball? You've been promising me for a long time."

"I can't today, Carlitos. I have a very important meeting that will take most of the afternoon," he said, checking his watch. "Some other day."

"How about if I go with you? I'll just watch."

His father started laughing. "No, I don't think so."

"Come on, Papi, don't you want me to learn by your example," Carlos said, his voice cracking, his fists on the table.

Mr. Fernández stopped laughing. For a long moment, he stared at his son suspiciously. Then without saying a word, he got up from the table and left the house.

In September, the Catholic Church, a powerful institution in this staunchly half-hearted religious country became alarmed by the Revolution's excesses, especially by Fidel's plan to confiscate the church's vast portfolio of properties throughout the island. The conflict quickly escalated with Fidel and the elderly cardinal of Havana trading jabs via frequent speeches in front of their respective audiences. The animosity reached the boiling point during a short three-and-one-half-hour speech Fidel gave before a crowd of over two hundred thousand people.

Luis' mother assured her son that every single one of them would end up burning in eternal hell. Luis worried that his father had been present at the rally.

On the twenty-ninth of September, close to a million faithful followers of the church, including Luis' mother, of course, gathered in Havana in support of the church with chants of "Social justice, yes! Communism, no!"

A law was swiftly instituted prohibiting any public demonstrations not specifically summoned by the Revolution, and the cardinal was invited to leave Cuba or all churches would be closed, indefinitely.

The next day Luis stepped out of the classroom of the exclusive private Catholic school he attended on a full scholarship, thanks to his mother's devout faith and exceptionally fine embroidery work that she regularly donated to the Church. The Jesuit priest who taught the nineteen boys in his class handed Luis a slip of paper.

"I want both your father's and mother's signature, young man." The priest's accent from Spain was pronounced and the tone of his voice inflicted mortal fear in every boy, except Luis, who stuffed the paper in his back pocket.

Outside on the asphalt playground, a group of boys, ages six through twelve years old, dressed in white shirts, navy-blue ties, short khaki pants, white socks, and black lace-up shoes, waited in neatly formed lines to board several school buses proudly displaying the school's logo of Jesus bleeding on the cross.

From Amigos to Friends

Luis was about to reach his bus when, between the heads of two boys in line in front of him, he spotted his father pulling up at the gate on his Harley-Davidson.

The Harley had come courtesy of the Revolution. More precisely, it came with the house Luis' father had "intervened" in the name of the Revolution when Carlos' next-door neighbor fled the country a week after Batista's departure.

Mr. Rodríguez wore a black beret and military fatigues with knee-high paratrooper boots. His beard was now full and peppered with grey. Luis madly waved his arms in the air. His father spotted him, revved up the Harley's muscular engine and waved for Luis to join him.

Without hesitation, Luis broke ranks. He ran to his father, jumped on the Harley, wrapped his arms around his father's waist, and the Harley burned rubber all the way to the corner, banked the curb and sped away. Luis looked over his shoulder and saw kids craning their heads out of the school buses. The priest in charge of the orderly departure of school buses chased the motorcycle down the middle of the street, yelling and wildly waving his arms in the air. Luis' heart pounded against his father's muscular back.

Speeding down Fifth Avenue, a wide boulevard lined with mansions and centered by a median covered with mature trees, Mr. Rodríguez suddenly turned his head and said, "Don't believe a word those fascist Jesuit priests tell you. They're a pack of liars."

"But, Papi..."

"I mean it, Luis. Not a word!"

As they approached their new home, Luis spotted his mother posted in front of the garage door with her arms tightly crossed. The Harley down-shifted and entered the long concrete driveway. The motorcycle aimed straight for his mother. She firmly held her ground. The brakes screeched. Luis shut his eyes and buried his face in his father's fatigues.

The Harley came to a sudden halt, throwing Luis tight against his father.

"Are you mad?" she shouted. "Are you crazy?" Mrs. Rodríguez ripped Luis off the motorcycle. "What do you think you're doing to your son?"

"Mami, all Papi did was pick me up from school."

"You! You're just like your father!" She smacked his behind. "Go inside the house right now!"

Luis ran toward the big house and went behind a blooming hibiscus hedge by the front porch. There he found his older sister hiding.

"You and Papi are in a lot of trouble," Elena said and laughed.

"What are you smiling about?" Mrs. Rodríguez yelled at her husband. "You have to follow rules and procedures just like everybody else. You can't just kidnap Luis from school!"

"Kidnap?"

"You heard me!"

"Luis is my son. I picked up my son from school. I didn't kidnap him!"

"You stole him! That's exactly the way the father superior said it."

"The father superior can go to hell where he belongs!" He pressed his heaving chest to within an inch of his wife.

She held her ground and shoved her husband out of her way. She looked up toward heaven and made the sign of the cross. "Don't be disrespectful. How do you expect the children to learn any morals with the way you behave?"

"They'll learn more and better morals from me than from those priests and nuns you send them to."

Luis and his sister ran into the house. Inside, Elena grinned and started humming a song.

"What are you so happy about?" Luis asked, knowing the answer.

From Amigos to Friends

"Mami really picked you and Papi apart," she said. "And both of you deserve it!"

"I hate you!" Luis pushed her to the floor and ran to his room.

Mr. Rodríguez marched through the living room toward his room. Right behind him, Mrs. Rodríguez stormed into the house and returned to her sewing machine. Volunteering additional hours for the diocese appeased the constant guilt she suffered from living in this house. During daily confessions, her confessor helped her with the forced compromise of living with the constant sin of residing in a house her husband had stolen in order to abide by and fulfill her wedding vow to obey her spouse.

Luis entered his parents' new bedroom and sat down next to his father, who was in the middle of struggling through his daily one hundred sit-ups. His father's intense black eyes reached his and then fell back to the floor.

Luis examined his father's full beard and balding head and wondered what he would look like when he turned forty, like his father.

"Luisito, are you doing sit-ups and pull-ups everyday?" his father asked, sitting up and staring into his son's eyes.

"Well I..." Luis started to lie, but changed his mind, not able to escape his father's judging eyes. "No, I'm not."

"Well you must! The Revolution needs strong young men!"

His mother appeared at the bedroom door. "Keep the Revolution to yourself and outside this house that doesn't belong to us," she said, crossing herself as if asking for forgiveness. "Come on, lunch is going to get cold."

Luis, his sister, and his mother sat at the dining room table and waited for Luis' father. Luis' stomach started aching the instant he sat down. It had been like this for months, since the beginning of the year. His parents' arguments had intensified daily as the friction, between "your Communist Revolution" as she described it and "your fascist Catholic

Church" as he retaliated, escalated exponentially. And during meals, the dining room table had become the center ring where rules, like not-hitting-below-the-belt or not-striking-when-the-opponent-is-down-for-a-mandatory-count-of-eight, had long been abandoned.

Mr. Rodríguez entered the dining room in his revolutionary fatigues, paratrooper boots, and black beret. At the head of the table, he took his place.

"Papi, you look just like Fidel," Elena said, looking down at her garbanzo bean soup and then discreetly at her mother's reaction.

Luis' stomach knotted.

"Thank you, that's quite a compliment," Mr. Rodríguez said, arranging his napkin to avoid staining his uniform.

"You look ridiculous," Mrs. Rodríguez frowned. "Why you dress like you're about to jump out of an airplane is beyond me."

"Mami, the soup is really good," Luis lied. "Papi, how fast can your motorcycle go?"

"I wear this uniform to commemorate the Revolution... as a symbol of the struggle of working men and women to achieve equality and to control their own destiny."

"Mami, Papi, do you think I'll get a bike this Christmas?" Luis asked.

"All I see is that uniform giving you license to take what's not yours." Mrs. Rodríguez made the sign of the cross and looked up toward heaven. "Please forgive us for living in this house that my husband stole, my Lord."

"Papi, how fast can the motorcycle go?" Luis repeated.

"Freedom, woman! Freedom! That's what the Revolution is all about. Freedom for every man, woman, and child to express their thoughts. Freedom to actualize their dreams. Freedom to..."

"You're an atheist... a clown," Mrs. Rodríguez said, interrupting her husband. "God will punish all of us for your mortal sins."

"Mami, Papi, I got in trouble at school," Luis said, waving the note from school. "I need both of you to sign this."

"That's it!" Mr. Rodríguez suddenly got up from his chair. His leg bumped the table, knocking over glasses and spilling yellow garbanzo bean soup all over the table. "I will not be called a clown. I will not put up with your insults another second. I'll never set foot in this house again, where I'm no longer respected!" He threw his napkin on the table and stormed out of the house.

Luis heard the Harley roar and then burn rubber.

Mrs. Rodríguez began cleaning the dining room table. "Who needs him?" she said. "We're better off without him!"

"I agree, Mami," Elena said.

"Be quiet! I didn't ask for your opinion," Mrs. Rodríguez said and then broke down in tears.

Luis ran to his new room, crying.

CHAPTER IV

January 1, 1960, heralded a fresh decade and launched the second year under the Revolution. It also marked a new period in the lives of the three boys. The anxiety they sensed all around them compelled them to listen to discussions that had been unimportant to them in the past. It opened their eyes to a wide range of subjects, from the political and social upheavals taking place within their country to the Presidential election campaign in the United States between Richard M. Nixon and John F. Kennedy.

In February, Anastas Mikoyan, vice-premier minister of the Soviet Union, arrived in Havana. Cuba and the Soviet Union signed an agreement whereby the Soviet government extended the Revolution one hundred million dollars of credit and committed to purchase one-fifth of the island's sugar production.

Several days of pomp and circumstance surrounded the historic event, including a parade of military tanks down Fifth Avenue that completely captured the imaginations of the three friends.

In March, the cargo ship La Coubre blew up while being unloaded in the Port of Havana. Its cargo of heavy weapons manufactured in the Soviet Union made news of the explosion difficult to keep quiet. David remembered studying in history class how back in 1898 the explosion of another ship in the same Port of Havana had triggered the Spanish-American War.

43

Fidel, an avid student of history, immediately pinned the cause of the explosion of the cargo ship squarely in the criminal hands of the CIA. In a series of inhumanly long, passionate speeches, the Maximum Leader painted a vivid parallel between the two events and predicted another imminent invasion of Cuba's white beaches by the United States Marines.

Luis' father cheered the Maximum Leader's speeches calling for every man, woman, and child to safeguard the Revolution—with their lives if necessary. The Revolution armed thousands of young men and women and mobilized them throughout the island, ready to confront and defeat "the imminent invasion by the United States Marines."

"Fatherland or death! We will be victorious!" Mr. Rodríguez taught his son Luis Fidel's new revolutionary slogan.

A month later, "as if to test the United States' limits," as Mr. Fernández explained it to his son Carlos, Fidel expropriated all American-owned properties on the island. During several blistering, marathon speeches, Fidel justified this radical, provocative move as a national security imperative.

Luis would remain neutral when listening to his parents' opposite-view tirades. His father would ramble on about how brave Fidel was seizing strategic properties from the evil, imperialistic giant from the north. When with his mother, Luis endured her scathing indictment of Castro as the personification of Satan, stealing from anyone in sight.

By the start of the school year, discontent was widespread in Cuba. The shortage of consumer products, from shoes to toilet paper and soap, was raising tempers. But most irritating of all was the shortage of food. It affected everyone, but most directly the poor, from whom the Revolution drew the most support.

Searching for a solution to the food shortages, the Maximum Leader created "Neighborhood Vigilance Committees." Within every few blocks in every neighborhood, a household was selected to observe, record, and inform on any suspicious act in the local households. A multitude of plots throughout the island were uncovered and announced by the Neighborhood Vigilance Committees. Some of these revelations culminated in the execution by firing squad of "counterrevolutionary worms."

Luis found his father exuberant when Fidel once more spoke to the country via a live televised speech and in thrilling detail unmasked a systematic network of CIA-driven sabotages as the real culprit for "the temporary shortages." This satanic network involved misguided Cubans. "Worms! Counterrevolutionaries!" The Revolution was not only in danger from the threat of a United States invasion, but it was now also threatened by these worms from within the island. Terror spread throughout Cuba.

The food shortages continued.

One crisp Saturday morning, David rode the three-speed bike his parents had bought him for his fourteenth birthday. It looked and felt brand new, even though a classmate had previously owned it. When David learned that Jorge had left for Miami, David convinced his parents to buy him the bike from Jorge's parents who had stayed behind in Cuba.

Jorge's mother had started crying when David climbed on the bike and took it for a spin. Jorge's mother could not stop crying and refused to take Mr. Oviedo's money. David's father insisted on paying for the bike. She repeated that he was doing her a favor by taking the bike because it hurt her to see it in the garage every day. But Mr. Oviedo insisted on paying for the bike, or he would not take it.

Pelayo "Pete" Garcia

David worried about leaving empty-handed and decided to close the deal by pedaling away as fast as he could. It wasn't brand new, but after searching in vain throughout the entire city of Havana for a new three-speed, David was thrilled with his almost-new red beauty.

David squeezed hard on the handlebar brakes, and his bike skidded to a stop in front of his father's old office. After a year of keeping the architectural office open without drawing a single line, Mr. Oviedo had converted it into a store that sold books, sports equipment, and toys. The ground floor space, well located on a busy Fifth Avenue corner, lent itself well to retail use, and after gutting the internal partitions and expanding the amount of glass on the front, the store had opened six weeks earlier.

The unusual mix of merchandise for sale was the result of what David's father had been able to procure. Mr. Oviedo kept the store open six days a week, Monday through Saturday from ten to eight. It closed for lunch between twelve and two. Mrs. Oviedo helped out in the mornings, and David worked on Saturdays.

David got bored sitting in front of the store waiting for his father and took off. The red machine accelerated as David shifted gears and disappeared, making a sharp turn at the corner. The fenders have to go, David decided. They slow me down too much. Pumped full of adrenaline, he made a daring U-turn and headed back to the store. He leaned over the handlebars, jumped on the pedals with all his weight and strength, and shifted big red into high gear. It was time to find out how fast it could go. It was fast. David was impressed. It was even faster than he had expected. Wait till I strip it down, he thought. The ringer, the fenders, the light, the bookrack in the back, they all have to go.

David had reached top speed when he spotted his mother getting out of her car in front of the store. He panicked. She saw her son coming toward her at a frightening speed and she panicked. David gripped the handlebar brakes with all his strength. The rubber pads squealed loudly against the wheels' metal rims, and his new racing machine came to a halt. Had he not been terrified of losing his bike after owning it less than a half-hour, he would have been impressed.

"Hi, Mami! How do you like it?" David said, trying not to sound totally out of breath.

Mrs. Oviedo stormed inside the building.

David entered the store and was immediately sent to the storage room, where he leaned the bike against the wall. He found a screwdriver and removed the ringer from the handlebar. They're talking about me, he thought. I wonder if they're arguing. He had never seen his parents argue. He had seen them disagreeing, but never arguing like Carlos' parents. And, thank God, never like he had seen Luis' parents abusing each other. When he heard the door opening, he quickly put the screwdriver back in the toolbox and threw the ringer into the trash can.

Mr. Oviedo entered the storage room. "Your mother tells me she caught you racing the bicycle," Mr. Oviedo said. "Son, it's important that you accept responsibility for your actions. You're not allowed to ride the bike for a week."

David lowered his eyes and nodded.

"It's probably the most important lesson I can teach you in life," his father said, resting his hand on David's shoulder.

"Yes, I understand."

After his father left the storage room, David sat on the concrete floor in front of his new bike. He stared at the bike and sulked.

"I had a long conversation with the lady who sold me the bicycle," David overheard his father say. "She and her husband sent their son to the United States."

With nothing else to do, David eavesdropped on his parents' conversation.

"To live with relatives?"

Pelayo "Pete" Garcia

"No..."

"They sent a fourteen-year-old to the United States by himself?" His mother said. "That's terrible!"

Intrigued, David listened with renewed interest.

"The Catholic Church has an organization that looks after the kids when they get to Miami."

"Why are you telling me this?"

"It's something we should talk about. Something maybe we should consider," his father said. "It may be the best thing for David's future."

David tried to imagine what it would be like to live in the United States. He had been to Miami with his parents several times. English only. Hamburgers and hot dogs everyday. A new school. New friends. Am I good enough to make the baseball team playing against American kids? I better be, or I'll never make it to the major leagues. What if I don't make it? Then what? Build bridges, roads, big buildings, the bigger the better. I'll be an engineer, different than father, but we could work together. I'm smart. I can get good grades in the United States. And Carlos and Luis? No problem. They'll end up in the United States.

On Valentine's Day, Carlos and his father sat on adjoining chairs at the barbershop. The barber had an assistant on Saturdays and he refrained from politics, concentrating on baseball instead.

The electric razor scraped Carlos' scalp, its loud buzzing giving him a headache. The weekly crew cut was mandatory at the Havana Military School where Carlos now attended the eighth grade. During his sister's graduation ceremonies the previous summer, the headmaster had informed his parents that the school refused to tolerate Carlos' behavior any longer. The headmaster proceeded to destroy Carlos' summer vacation by suggesting that his parents' only hope was to enroll

Carlos in a military school where he would be under the strictest discipline possible. Carlos' sole consolation was that he had ruined his sister's graduation.

"I've cornered the market," Carlos heard his father say in a low voice meant to be heard only by the barber cutting his father's hair. "I own more General Motors cars than anybody on the island."

"You know, I've always wanted a two-tone Chevy," the barber said.

"I bought them for pràctically nothing," Mr. Fernández bragged, looking at himself in the mirror.

"How much would a '55 Chevy go for?" the barber asked, sharpening the razor on the leather belt hanging behind the chair.

"I'm a genius, that's what I am. A genius," Mr. Fernández bragged, admiring himself in the mirror while the barber trimmed his sideburns with the razor. "Before the government made it illegal, I bought my neighbors' cars for a few pesos as they left for Miami. Brother, when the word got around that I was buying, I was able to buy so many cars that I've run out of space at the dealership."

"If you bought them so cheap, maybe I can afford to buy one from you," the barber said as he turned Mr. Fernández's face from side to side to make sure the sideburns were even.

"Hey, no way. I'm waiting to resell them for top prices," Mr. Fernández said. "I'm not doing this for the sport of it."

"How can you do that?" the barber asked. He stuck two fingers in a jar of Vaseline, rubbed the oily paste on the palm of his hands, and plastered Mr. Fernández's few remaining hairs to his scalp.

"When Fidel falls and they come back from Miami," Mr. Fernández explained with a grin on his face, "I'll sell them their own cars back for ten times what I paid them."

The barber carefully and meticulously spread out with a comb the few hairs on top of Mr. Fernández's head, trying to cover as much of the scalp as possible. "They may not come back for awhile," the barber pointed out.

"Nah," Mr. Fernández said. "It's a matter of weeks."

"Or maybe years," the barber said, prophetically.

Mr. Fernández tipped his head, signaling the barber to come closer. "The Marines are landing before this summer," he whispered. "Shoulder to shoulder with a brigade of Cubans trained by the Marines."

"Rumors," the barber pointed out. "If we had as much food as rumors, we wouldn't need the Marines." He brushed off the back of Mr. Fernández's neck and then took off the sheet.

"You heard it right here. From the General Motors King," Mr. Fernández said. "I've been told that *The New York Times* has confirmed that the invasion will be in a matter of weeks."

"I'll believe it when a Marine is sitting in this chair getting a crew cut," the barber said, taking the money from Carlos' father. He grinned, noticing the extravagant nature of the tip, and with a brush he attentively dusted the King's shoulders.

On their way to the Cadillac, the father and son walked past Carlos' favorite store: the Miramar Record Shop. Painted on the shop's storefront was a giant red heart engulfing a couple kissing. A Valentine's Day sale was in effect.

"Have you bought Mami a Valentine's Day present?" Carlos asked, dashing inside the store.

Mr. Fernández reluctantly entered the store and asked a salesclerk where to find Frank Sinatra. Carlos darted for the rock-and-roll section.

Carlos narrowed his choice to Elvis' "Jail House Rock" and "G. I. Blues" LPs. He knew that he had a pretty good chance of manipulating his father into buying one, but not both. He saw his father approach the cash register with a record. "Think, Carlos. Think," he mumbled on his way to meet his father.

"Papi, can I get one? Please."

From Amigos to Friends

"Good idea, Carlitos. Pick one out. Take your time," his father said, waving him away from the cash register.

"How about one for my sister?"

"Sure, sure. Go pick one out for your sister. Go on."

Carlos smiled. He headed to the rock-and-roll rack and turned back to see the salesclerk slip two records into a shopping bag that he then handed to his father. Carlos wasted a couple of minutes and returned to the counter with the two Elvis Presley records.

Mr. Fernández looked at the covers. "I thought your sister didn't like Elvis Presley?"

"No, she likes him," Carlos lied.

When they reached the Cadillac, Mr. Fernández insisted on putting both shopping bags in the trunk. They had barely sat in the car when his father suddenly said, "Wait here, Carlitos." Mr. Fernández got out of the car and took both bags out of the trunk.

They drove down Fifth Avenue toward their house. Carlos looked in the shopping bags. "Papi, you're missing a record," Carlos pointed out.

"What do you mean?" Mr. Fernández wrinkled his forehead.

"Your bag. I saw the clerk put two records in your bag, but now there's only one," Carlos said, suspiciously.

"Yeah, well, don't worry about it," Mr. Fernández said with parental authority and turned on the radio.

"But where's the other record?" Carlos insisted.

"In the trunk. Be quiet, I want to listen to the news," Mr. Fernández said and raised the volume.

"Who's the record for?"

"It's for my secretary. She's been working very hard these days and I thought I'd do something nice for her."

"What's her name?"

"Her name is Linda," his father said after a long pause. His fair skin had turned beet red.

Carlos felt his body shiver and his fists tighten. "Does Mami know about her?" Carlos asked, his voice cracking.

"What kind of a question is that?"

"Does she?"

The Cadillac picked up speed.

"What kind of question is that?" his father repeated, this time in a more accusing tone.

The Cadillac pulled into the driveway and stopped. Mr. Fernández grabbed Carlos' arm. "Answer me, damn it!"

Carlos shook his arm loose, jumped out of the car, and dashed toward the house. Carlos passed his mother on the stairs, bolted into his room, and slammed the door behind him. His mother went into his room and found Carlos lying in bed with his face buried in a pillow.

His mother sat on the edge of the bed next to him. "Did you get into an argument with your father?"

Carlos got out of bed and went to the door. "Mami, it was nothing," he said. "I have to go feed Rocky." Carlos left the room and ran downstairs.

Mr. Fernández entered the house as his wife came out of her son's room. They met halfway up the stairs.

"Where is he?" Mr. Fernández demanded to know.

"He's out feeding the dog."

Wrong. Carlos was listening in on their conversation, hoping that his mother would find out about his father and kick him out of their lives.

"What did he say to you?" he asked, suspiciously.

"Let's go in the bedroom," she said. "We have to talk!"

Carlos' father followed his wife into their bedroom. She closed the door behind them. Carlos crept to the door and very quietly cracked the door open just enough to hear their conversation.

"I'm very upset!" she said, firmly placing her hands on her abundant hips.

"What did he say to you?" he asked with concern.

"We must leave the country at once!"

"That's not going to solve anything." Resigned to admit his affair, he sat down on a Louis XVI chair.

"We must do what is best for the children's futures." She sat on a chair across from him, a defeated look on her face.

"I agree," he confessed. "We must isolate them from the whole affair. I..."

"I'm relieved that you agree with me," she interrupted. "If we don't isolate her, she's going to get herself and the rest of us into a lot of trouble."

"That won't be a problem," he said. "I'll move..."

"If we don't, we'll all be at the mercy of those bearded bandits," she said, looking toward heaven and respectfully making the sign of the cross.

"What are you talking about?" he asked, confused.

"Your daughter," she said. "That's who I'm talking about."

"What does she have to do with this?"

"I found counterrevolutionary leaflets hidden under her bed!"

"My daughter? The bookworm?" he said, suddenly relieved and yet concerned.

"She's not a bookworm. She's not only very smart, she's a leader. She was senior class president."

"That's different."

"No, it's not," she disagreed. "She's associating with a group of students at the university who are plotting against the government."

"She's only eighteen years old," he said, dismissing his wife's concern.

"Well, that's how old the Ramírez's boy is," she reminded him, "and you know the story. One day the militia picked him up at his house in the middle of the night and now he's serving a twenty-year sentence for counterrevolutionary activities."

"Well, leaving the country is not the answer," he said, standing up and pacing the room. "Discipline and respect for her parents is the answer. Besides, this Revolution won't last much longer. The Ramírez's boy will be out on the street in a few weeks."

"You've never understood her. She's..."

He cut her off. "Just because I didn't go to college doesn't mean that I can't understand what she's going through," he said. "I'll take care of it. I'll straighten her out."

"Don't be hard on her!"

Carlos slipped back into his room as Mr. Fernández stepped into the hallway, followed by his wife.

━━━━

Returning home after spending a full day at the television station with his father, Luis dismounted the Harley.

"Papi, why don't you come in and have a cup of coffee or something?"

"I have to run, son. I'll see you soon."

"When?"

"Soon."

"How soon?"

"Luisito, I have a lot on my mind. I'll call you."

Luis lowered his head and moved away.

"Luisito," his father said. "Ask your mother to come out here and talk to me for a minute."

Luis rushed inside the house with a smile on his face and found his mother bent over her sewing machine.

"Mami! Mami! Papi wants you to come outside and talk to him!"

His mother primped, looking at herself in a small mirror hanging on the wall. She arranged her hair and said, "Go tell your father that if he wants to talk to me, he has to come in the house."

From Amigos to Friends

Luis frowned. "Please, you know he won't come in," he said. "He's in a bad mood. I don't want to upset him anymore."

Hiding behind the hibiscus bush, Luis sat down to listen in on his parent's conversation.

Mrs. Rodríguez reached the sidewalk and, crossing her arms, planted herself in front of her husband. "It would be a lot more comfortable inside the house," she pointed out. "If you come in, I promise you I won't insult you."

He reached out to give her a handful of cash. She recoiled as if he were handing her the keys to the gates of hell. "I don't need your stolen money."

"I didn't ask you to come out here to fight," he said, turning very serious. "You have to stop attending meetings at the church."

She laughed. "Is this some kind of joke, or have you finally lost your mind?"

"It's important."

"What could possibly make me do that?" she asked, placing her hands firmly on her hips.

"You have to. Trust me. That's all I can say."

"You're serious, aren't you?" she said, recognizing fear in his eyes.

"This is one time you have to back off. It's not safe."

"What are they going to do? Torture me?"

"The Revolution is very sensitive right now to subversive activities."

"A bunch of women meeting with a priest to pray and plan community services?"

"The Catholic Church is only using you. What they really want to do is overthrow the Revolution."

"Well, you can forget it," she said, turning toward the house.

He gripped her arm. "Woman, don't be stubborn. You're endangering yourself and the children."

She pulled away from him. "Is that a threat?" she asked with fury in her eyes. "If it is, you can go right now and never come back here ever again."

"Calm down, woman," he began, fearfully looking all around him to make sure nobody was listening. "You can't repeat any of this to anyone or I'll be in serious trouble. Agreed?"

"Go on," she said reluctantly.

"The Revolution is putting together a list of anybody who can potentially be dangerous to the Revolution."

"How can you be involved with all this?" she said, accusingly. "Not even Batista went that far."

"We fought hard for this Revolution and we're not going to lose it."

"So you're part of this evil plan," she said, crossing herself. "How could I have ever married you?"

"I'm not a monster," he said, defending himself. "I'm doing this for the people."

"Please, don't try to sound like Fidel. It's bad enough that you try to look like him."

"This is not the time to insult each other," he said, containing his temper. "I'm not threatening you. I'm simply warning you because I care. If you keep hanging around the church, you're branding yourself and the kids as enemies of the Revolution. I don't expect you to like it or agree with it, but that's the reality of the situation."

She remained quiet for a long moment. They stared at each other with mixed feelings. "Do you want to stay for dinner? We're having chicken and rice."

"No, but thanks for asking." He jumped on the kick start, revved up the engine, and left.

Mrs. Rodríguez caught Luis hiding behind the hibiscus bush. She shook a finger at him, and he followed her into the house.

"Are you and Papi getting back together again?" Luis asked.

"We will some day."

Luis smiled. "I had a great time at the television station. It was really exciting. When I grow up, I want to be like Papi."

"Come and tell me all about it," she said, going into the kitchen to check on the yellow rice simmering on the stove.

"When are you and Papi going to make up so we can all live together again?" Luis' sister asked as she followed her mother and brother into the kitchen.

Luis smiled.

doom is a miracle, Luis concluded. And having attended Catholic school since kindergarten, he knew that escaping a bad report card was insufficient grounds for a miracle. But he prayed for one, just in case.

━━━━━

When he first heard the airplanes, David's watch marked exactly six in the morning. The room vibrated with the roar of the engines. Two, three, maybe more. They came from the ocean and flew over his house so low it seemed as if they were coming in through the window, heading in the direction of the military airport several miles inland. David's heart began pounding against his chest. His brother started crying. He had lived in this house all his life and had never experienced airplanes like that—not even close.

The first explosion rocked the house. The mirror hanging over David's dresser crashed on the black marble floor and shattered into a thousand pieces. David's ears rang as more and more bombs exploded. He leaped from his bed and landed past the broken glass. He ran into his brother's room, swooped the hysterically crying toddler from his crib and ran toward his parents' bedroom. In the hallway, he ran into them, still in their pajamas.

"In the kitchen!" Mr. Oviedo yelled. "Run to the kitchen!"

Another series of explosions shook the house. They ran down the hallway toward the kitchen as pictures fell from the walls all around them. Machine-gun fire now filled the time between explosions. María, with tears streaming down her face, stood paralyzed in the middle of the kitchen.

Mr. Oviedo shoved everyone into the walk-in pantry. It was a tight fit for all five of them. In David's arms, the toddler cried hysterically. Mrs. Oviedo took the toddler from David.

"They're bombing the airfield. This room is the safest in the house. It has the most walls around it," Mr. Oviedo explained as if he had planned for such an event long ago. He

closed the heavy wood door and flipped a light switch. A raw
60-watt bulb illuminated five terrified faces.

"Papi, is it the Marines?" David asked, excitedly.

"I don't know, son. I don't know."

David's brother screamed at the top of his lungs, drowning out the machine-gun fire.

"Open the door!" Mrs. Oviedo pleaded. "He won't be so
scared with some daylight."

A series of consecutive blasts climaxed in one huge explosion that threatened to separate the house from its foundation.

The room went dark.

The rumbling of airplane engines got closer and closer.
Machine-gun fire was deafening, and intermittent explosions
sounded in the background.

"I think the planes are headed back our way," Mr. Oviedo
said. "Everybody on the floor!"

At that moment, the toddler stopped crying, and, as if in
the eye of a hurricane, the tiny room became perfectly calm.
The planes flew over the house, vibrating cans and bottles off
the shelves and onto the tops of their heads. Antiaircraft
artillery exploded over the house, and the light suddenly came
on.

Mr. Oviedo threw himself protectively over his wife and
two sons. María held on to David.

———

At Carlos' house, with plaster dust all over his pajamas,
Mr. Fernández was the first one to get up from his bedroom
floor. Alicia sprang to her feet and ran out of the room. Mrs.
Fernández held onto her son, who held onto Rocky, who would
not stop howling.

Carlos finally wiggled loose from his mother's grip and
ran out of the room with Rocky close on his heels. He reached
the kitchen and found the maid and Susie huddled in a cor-

ner. He helped the maid off of the floor and then chased Susie around the kitchen, trying to catch the old hen.

Alicia ran down the stairs, putting on her clothes.

Mr. Fernández and his wife rushed to the top of the stairs. "Where do you think you're going?" they yelled simultaneously.

Alicia froze ten steps from the front door. "I'm going to meet some friends," she said without looking back and made a mad dash for the front door. Mr. Fernández bolted and reached his daughter faster than Carlos had ever seen his father move. He plucked his daughter off her feet, slammed the door shut, and dragged the struggling teenager up the stairs.

"Let me go!" she screamed. "It's time for action. The invasion is happening!"

"Be careful, don't hurt her," Mrs. Fernández pleaded, following her husband up to their daughter's bedroom.

"You stay in your room till I say so!" her father ordered and slammed the door shut.

"Papi, please, it's my duty!" Alicia pleaded, pounding on her door.

Mr. Fernández towered over his wife. "You make sure she doesn't leave her room," he said, threatening his wife. "She's going to get us all killed before the Marines take control. Stupid girl!"

"She's just young and idealistic," Mrs. Fernández said in tears and then slipped into her daughter's room.

Mr. Rodríguez ran into the house and found his wife and children with their hair and pajamas covered with plaster dust, peacefully sitting at the dining room table, drinking from empty cups. The chandelier had fallen from the ceiling and lay on top of the table in broken pieces. The few pictures left on the walls hung crookedly.

"Would you like some coffee?" Mrs. Rodríguez calmly offered her estranged husband. "I'm sorry it's cold, but the electricity went out."

Mr. Rodríguez helped his wife out of her chair. "You look very tired, dear," he said. "Let me help you get into bed."

In their bedroom, Mr. Rodríguez helped his wife lie down. As he sat on the edge of the bed next to her, caressing her forehead, she fell asleep. "No matter what happens, we'll get through it together," he said, kissed her lips and left.

When his father returned to the dining room, Luis said, "Papi, I knew something was wrong with Mami because right after the planes left, she told me to hurry up and get dressed because she didn't want me to be late for school."

<hr />

Just before lunch, two military jeeps screeched to a halt in front of David's house, and soldiers armed with automatic weapons stormed the house. David spotted the soldiers while doing chin-ups from the clothesline bar in the back yard. In the kitchen, David found a young soldier leaning against the kitchen counter, demanding a cup of coffee from María. Another soldier was hovering over eggs frying in a pan next to a pressure cooker hissing steam up to the ceiling. A third soldier was riffling through the refrigerator.

"Hey, put that back!" David ordered, catching the soldier taking a chocolate cake out of the refrigerator.

The soldier glanced down at David and laughed. María ushered David out of the kitchen into the living room. Out of the corner of his eye, David spotted two soldiers at the end of the hall, posted at the doorway to his parents' bedroom. A chill crawled up his back. María held him, but he struggled out of her arms and ran to his parents' bedroom. The soldiers blocked the entrance, and between their broad shoulders, David spotted a menacing black machine gun on top of his mother's embroidered, linen bedspread. Then he witnessed a soldier emptying the drawers from his mother's nightstand onto the floor. His parents nervously sat on the far edge of their bed. His mother held his brother tightly in her arms. An officer towered over them, accusingly shoving a piece of paper in front of their faces.

"Where's your sixteen-year-old son?" the officer asked, consulting a list of names.

"He's only fourteen," Mr. Oviedo replied.

"He just turned fourteen," Mrs. Oviedo added.

"I have orders to arrest all three of you."

David pushed himself past the soldiers. "I'm here," he announced, squaring off in front of the officer.

The officer sized up David's five-foot-one, one-hundred-pound frame and said, "Fourteen? He looks more like twelve to me. He doesn't look very dangerous."

The soldiers laughed. David frowned.

"That's what you think!" David threatened.

"David, be quiet!" his parents simultaneously scolded him.

The officer reached to take David's brother from his mother. She slid back and hung onto the toddler, who started to cry.

"Please don't take my wife and son," Mr. Oviedo pleaded. "If you only take me, they won't even leave the house."

"We haven't done anything!" she protested.

A soldier came into the room. "Sir, we haven't found anything. The house is clean."

"What's all over your mouth?" The officer asked one of the soldiers.

"Chocolate cake," David said, accusingly.

"What are you searching for?" Mr. Oviedo asked.

"Weapons, propaganda, subversive material," the officer responded.

"You're wasting your time," Mr. Oviedo assured the officer. "We're peaceful citizens. We're not political."

The officer grabbed Mr. Oviedo's arm and brought him to his feet. "If you are, you'll be back. If you're lying, you won't."

Mrs. Oviedo started to get up, but the officer pushed her down. "It's your lucky day, lady. I'm going to take a chance and leave you here with your kids," he said and shoved Mr. Oviedo out of the bedroom.

David grabbed onto his father. "Where are you taking my father?" he demanded to know.

The officer jerked David away from his father and threw him onto the bed next to his mother.

Mrs. Oviedo clutched both of her sons.

Immediately after the bombing stopped, Mr. Fernández began ripping his house apart, searching madly and finding counterrevoluthout materials hidden all throughout the house. He turned up leaflets, flyers, newsletters, flags, autographed photos of the cardinal. Carlos ran back and forth to the garage with the incriminating evidence and piled it into a large tin tub they had used to wash clothes by hand before the arrival of a washing machine. Mrs. Fernández followed her husband, immediately putting the house back as it was before. Mr. Fernández had given the tearful maid the day off. Their daughter screamed to be released from her room the entire time.

"Let me out!" she protested. "I have to help bring down this atheist government! You don't have any right to kidnap me like this!"

At one point her father ripped open her bedroom door, grabbed his daughter's shoulders, and shook her violently. "This is not a game! You're putting your whole family in danger!"

Mrs. Fernández cuddled her daughter after her husband stormed out of the room to resume tearing the house apart.

From Amigos to Friends

After every nook and cranny was checked and double-checked, Carlos and his father went into the garage, poured gasoline siphoned out of the Cadillac over the incriminating material and set a match to the two-foot-high stack of what could have been front-row tickets to the firing squad. After every piece of paper was reduced to ashes, Carlos and his father scattered them throughout the back yard and washed away any remaining trace of evidence with a garden hose.

Carlos sat in the dining room with his mother and father. They ate ham and cheese sandwiches while Alicia carried on upstairs. Rocky started barking loudly in the back yard, where he was chained to the mango tree. Suddenly, the front door flew open and a bearded soldier, aiming an assault rifle, burst into the living room. Then two more soldiers stormed inside the house. Carlos sank down in his chair. Over his shoulder, he spotted another soldier crawling into the house through the kitchen window. Rocky barked so loud, Carlos worried that his dog would choke to death attempting to pull the giant mango tree out of the ground in an effort to come to his rescue. The kitchen door flew off its hinges and three soldiers burst inside. Mr. Fernández sprang up, his chair crashing to the floor. A formidable voice erupted out of his mouth. "What the hell are you doing in my house?"

The soldiers converged around the dining table, aiming their weapons at Mr. Fernández. "You move and you're dead!" a bearded soldier threatened as he stuck the barrel of his machine gun in Mr. Fernández's gut.

"This is my house!" Mr. Fernández protested, but not as loudly as before. "What's this all about?"

"Your daughter," the bearded officer said, lowering his rifle and motioning his soldiers to go search the house.

Mrs. Fernández covered her mouth, gasped, and then fainted. Carlos reached her and prevented her from falling off the chair.

Mr. Fernández quickly moved around the table and valiantly planted himself directly in front of the dark barrel of an assault rifle. "My daughter is eighteen years old! What do you want her for?" he asked with authority.

"She's suspected of counterrevolutionary activities," the bearded officer said, accusingly.

"Ridiculous!" Mr. Fernández quickly responded.

"Hey, isn't this the guy that sells cars on television?" one of the soldiers said with a smile as he dragged Alicia into the kitchen. The others also started smiling, including the bearded leader.

"In the flesh, gentlemen," Mr. Fernández said proudly, returning the smile.

"We're going to have to search the house, sir," the leader said apologetically and motioned for his men to proceed. "Let go of the young lady."

"Please, be my guest," Mr. Fernández replied, confidently. "Search the house."

Mrs. Fernández recovered and went to her daughter. She took her by the hand, and they sat down in the dining room under the crucifix.

"Captain, can I offer you a beer while your men do their patriotic duty?" Mr. Fernández offered.

"I'm just a lieutenant. I..."

"Well, lieutenant, by the way you handle your soldiers, I would've bet a hundred pesos you were at least a captain," Carlos' father said, acting surprised. "Please, sit down. Carlitos, get a couple of beers from the refrigerator."

After sneaking into the back yard to reassure Rocky that he was okay, Carlos returned with two cold bottles of Hatuey beer just as his father was delivering the punch line to the funniest dirty joke in his extensive repertoire. The young lieutenant almost fell off his chair laughing.

Now on a roll, Mr. Fernández handed the lieutenant a bottle of beer and said, "Lieutenant, how many Marines does it take to unscrew a light bulb?"

Still roaring from the last joke, the young officer drank from his bottle of beer and then said, "I have no idea."

"Five Marines."

"Five?"

"Yeah, one to hold the light bulb and four to turn the ladder!"

Both men cracked up.

Carlos faked a laugh. He had heard his father tell that joke a dozen times, using blacks, women, or Chinese instead, depending on his audience and their prejudices.

"Lieutenant, what kind of car do you drive?"

"Oh, I don't own a car, sir."

"Why not? A man of your stature deserves a car."

"I can't afford one, sir," he said humbly.

Mr. Fernández fished a business card out of his wallet and handed it to the young officer. "You come see me tomorrow, and I'll personally design a payment plan to work for you. You have my personal guarantee!" Carlos' father said, just like he did at the end of his television commercials.

Two soldiers approached the lieutenant and Mr. Fernández. "Sir, we haven't found anything," the taller one said, disappointed.

"Men, I hope you haven't made too much of a mess," Mr. Fernández said, "my wife is very proud of our house."

"Have you left the house the way you found it?" the lieutenant asked his men, sternly.

"Don't worry about it, lieutenant. You and your men have more important things to do." Mr. Fernández stood up and motioned for the lieutenant to accompany him to the front door.

The lieutenant stood up and followed Mr. Fernández. "Your daughter... I must..."

"Please, lieutenant. Don't worry about it," Mr. Fernández interrupted. "A simple case of mistaken identity. It's perfectly understandable."

"No, sir, I have to..."

"Lieutenant, please," Mr. Fernández insisted, reaching the front door. "You don't have to apologize."

"But..."

"I insist. Please, no apologies," Carlos' father said and opened the front door. "And to be on the safe side, I'll keep my daughter locked up in her room until I hear from you, lieutenant."

The soldiers filed outside. The lieutenant hesitated and then said, "That's a good idea, sir. I'll see you tomorrow." He turned around and stepped outside with Mr. Fernández's card in his hand.

Mr. Fernández closed the front door, let out a long sigh and said, "Carlitos, go get us a couple more cold beers."

***

Outside, the young bearded officer regrouped his soldiers and they moved next door, storming down the long driveway. They stopped to admire the Harley parked in front of the green garage door. After a brief argument about the Harley's top speed, the lieutenant huddled with his soldiers and began instructing them how to storm the house.

Luis and his father spotted them from the living room window and stepped outside. "May I help you, lieutenant?" Mr. Rodríguez offered.

The lieutenant looked up at Luis' father, who was wearing his paratroopers' uniform. The lieutenant sprang to his feet, saluted and said, "Captain, sir. I'm here to arrest a woman who lives in this house for counterrevolutionary activities, sir."

"At ease, lieutenant," Mr. Rodríguez said, returning the salute. "On your way, soldier. My men have taken her away.

I'm waiting for her relatives to arrive to take away the children." He turned and pointed at Luis standing next to him.

"Yes, sir!" The lieutenant saluted again. He then turned around, reviewed a list of names and addresses and marched his men down the sidewalk of the quiet neighborhood.

"Papi, I didn't know you were a captain," Luis whispered.

"Luisito, let's go inside and check on your mother."

Every hour of the day while his father remained missing, David sat in front of the television, which broadcasted reports and updates on the invasion by fifteen hundred Cubans who had landed at the Bay of Pigs, and were now being thrashed by the Revolution's troops. David tried to keep his thoughts positive, but the anguish was difficult to contain. He stared at the television and thought of his father.

What would it be like to not see him every day? To leave for school without his daily hug and kiss. Please, God, don't let anything happen to him. He's good. He's never done anything wrong to anyone. Why pick him to get hurt when there are so many bad people around. I'll promise you anything to get him back. Not only for me. How about my poor mother? And my brother will grow up without even remembering him. It's not fair. It's not fair! I know you won't do this to us. He'll be back. He'll be back. Please bring him back. Please. I miss him a lot.

On the fourth evening after his father's arrest, David and his mother ate dinner in complete silence. His brother sat next to his mother, constantly wiggling in his highchair.

"David, get your elbows off the table and sit up straight!" she said.

David slowly obeyed his mother while staring at the pineapple and cream cheese salad in front of him. His shoulders slumped forward and his arms hung down the sides of the chair.

"Mami, Mami," David's brother said, drooling.

"What sweetheart?" she replied, wiping his chin.

"Where's Papi?"

David buried his face in his hands.

María entered the dining room and placed in front of David an old bottle of watered-down catsup, a plate piled high with french fries, and a minuscule breaded steak. "This will make him feel better," she said, gently patting David's shoulders.

David pushed the plate away. "I don't want it! Leave me alone!" he said, moving his shoulders away from María.

"Mami, Mami, when is Papi coming back?"

David sprang from his chair. "Shut up!" he screamed at his brother at the top of his lungs.

"You shut up!" Mrs. Oviedo screamed at her older son.

David's brother started crying. María quickly left for the kitchen. David's mother slumped back on her chair and started to cry.

Seeing his mother cry for the first time in his life, David went to her and put his arms around her. "I'm sorry, Mami. I'm sorry."

They stopped crying on hearing the sound of keys working the lock on the front door. They stared as the door swung open, and Mr. Oviedo stepped over the threshold, scanning the living room as if seeing it for the first time. He found his family and reached out his arms toward them. David ran into his arms. Mrs. Oviedo reached them and they hugged, squeezing David between them. David opened his eyes and saw his mother's fair, soft skin tightly pressed against his father's four-day-old black beard.

They heard footsteps and voices approaching the wide-open front door. Carlos and Luis, followed by their entire families, entered the house.

The boys then sat on the living room floor and tuned into their parents' conversation.

From Amigos to Friends

"From here," Mr. Oviedo began, "they took me along to arrest three other men in the neighborhood. Gonzales the cardiologist, Avetrani the contractor and Pérez the barber. They drove us to an abandoned house in the Laguito area.

Mrs. Oviedo arrived with demi-tazze cups of steaming Cuban coffee on a silver tray. Mrs. Fernández moved several framed family photographs from a granite coffee table to make room for the coffee tray, and the conversation ceased while everyone reached for a cup.

"A textbook case of group psychological torture," Mrs. Rodríguez proclaimed, staring at her husband dressed in a smart olive-green paratrooper outfit.

The conversation captivated the boys to the point of allowing their sisters to share their space. María appeared with cups of hot chocolate for them.

"With this invasion over with, the country will settle down," Mr. Rodríguez proclaimed in defense of the Revolution. "There's plenty of work to do to make our country a better place for everyone, not just the rich and privileged class."

"Oh, please," his wife quickly responded, "let's spare the poor man from any more pain. He's been illegally detained and psychologically tortured for days."

"We were invaded. Under martial law these things happen," her husband said, defending his position.

"You're not going to get much support from this group," Mr Fernández said.

Luis' father stood up. "It's better if I leave," he said, setting his cup on the table and moving toward the front door.

David noticed Luis' jaw tighten. Carlos smiled.

Mr. Oviedo intercepted him. "Please, stay. You are a guest in our house."

Both men smiled and sat down.

"The second day was the worst," Mr. Oviedo began. "The soldiers guarding us were very nervous and restless. By nightfall an officer in his early fifties had all of us lined up against a wall..."

"How many prisoners were there?" Mr. Fernández asked.

"Thirty-six of us. I counted them. All men. Not all rich and privileged either," he said, addressing Luis' father, "but men from all walks of life. There was a tailor, a barber, a teacher, you name it. And not all of them white either. There were three blacks and one Chinese. Where was I?"

"Lined up against the wall," his wife said, sitting next to her husband and holding his arm.

"This officer and four very young soldiers armed with machine guns positioned themselves in front of us. I've never been so scared in my life. I thought this was the end. I could hear heavy breathing all around me. We were informed that a small number of Cuban exiles that had landed at the Bay of Pigs were surrounded and were ready to surrender. 'No Marines are involved,' the officer said with a huge grin. I'll never, as long as I live, forget the look on his face. He then told us that President Kennedy had announced that the United States would not get involved. He told us that we should be glad that Fidel's victory was assured. Because, otherwise, his orders were to kill every single one of us."

Everyone in the room gasped.

"Assassins!" Mrs. Rodríguez said to her husband.

David's father, now sitting at the edge of the couch, added, "The officer then called out a name and ordered the person to step forward. The man next to me, he was the oldest of the group, in his late sixties, tried to step forward. He shook from head to toe. He finally raised his hand. The soldiers then quickly plucked the old man from right next to me and forced the poor soul into a back room."

"Barbarians!" Mrs. Rodríguez said, staring at her husband.

From Amigos to Friends

David's father took a sip of coffee and continued, "Nobody slept that night. Wrapped in blankets, we lay on a cold marble floor. Thirty-six men in a room smaller than this living room."

Mesmerized, everyone looked around the room.

"What happened to the old man?" Mrs. Fernández asked from the edge of her seat, tears on her cheeks.

"They brought him back out after about an hour," Mr. Oviedo answered. "He was so frightened that he lost his voice. The officer came out of the back room and called out another name. It wasn't until the third man came back out from the back room that we found out what was going on."

David noticed that his father was shaking and his mother tried to comfort him.

"Please, take a break..."

"I'm all right," Mr. Oviedo assured Mrs. Fernández. "To terrorize us, they had intimidated them not to tell the rest of us what took place in the back room. The barber finally revealed that everyone of us would end up in the back room and go through a grueling interrogation. Not a comforting prospect, but it was better than the anxiety of not knowing."

"How many men were tortured?" Mrs. Rodríguez asked, staring at her husband.

"Nobody was tortured," David's father said.

"Are you sure of that?" she said, giving her smiling husband a dirty look.

"Nobody was physically hurt, but many of us have aged several years in the past four days," Mr. Oviedo pointed out.

"Your father is a brave man," Carlos' sister said to David.

"The rumor is that they arrested close to a million people throughout the island," Mrs. Oviedo told her husband.

"I don't believe for a minute the Americans have abandoned us," Mr. Fernández said. "You don't really think they're going to allow a Communist country ninety miles from their shore, do you?"

"Please, let's leave politics aside and talk about what we're going to do with these kids," Mrs. Oviedo said.

"We're not sure this is over with," David's father said.

"Can you imagine?" his wife said. "If what happened four days ago had happened with the kids at school?"

"I would've died," Carlos' mother said, looking toward her son with her hand over her mouth.

"What are you getting at?" Luis' mother asked.

The boys exchanged inquisitive looks.

"Before they took me away," Mr. Oviedo said, gazing at his wife and affectionately squeezing her hand, "we had decided not to send David back to school."

"He would be safer here at home," his wife added. "In case things flare up again."

David smiled. Carlos and Luis turned green with envy.

"An excellent idea," Mrs. Fernández said. "I'm keeping Carlos and his sister at home."

David and Carlos smiled. Luis frowned.

Alicia popped out of her chair. "Mother, that's ridiculous!" she said. "I have to go back to the university right away!"

Mr. Fernández suddenly stood up, and his daughter immediately sat back down. Luis wrinkled his forehead, soliciting comments. Both Carlos and David shrugged their shoulders.

"It's the end of April," Mr. Oviedo pointed out. "Summer is almost here anyway."

Mr. Fernández addressed Mr. Rodríguez. "It's the prudent thing to do."

"I'll go along with it for the rest of this year," Luis' father said, "but only because it gets my children out of those schools run by hypocrite, fascist priests and nuns."

Everyone in the room laughed except for Mrs. Rodríguez.

CHAPTER VI

Despite the turbulence and chaos all around them in their country, the three friends managed to go to the beach one balmy day. A breeze, heavily scented with saltwater, rustled the coconut trees that lined the shore. Calm, crystal clear Caribbean waters softly lapped at the fine, white sand. The sky was a playful gathering of cumulus clouds backed by a deep blue sky.

At the water's edge, with the surf intermittently caressing their feet, the boys spit on their masks and slowly rubbed the saliva against the glass, washing it off with seawater, as they had seen in the movies. Sitting in water up to their belly buttons, they slipped on their fins and then stood up with the ocean at their backs, preparing to venture out. Donning their masks and shoving the snorkels in their mouths, they valiantly began moving backward toward deeper water.

"David! Yoo-hoo!" They heard a girl's voice calling. "David!"

They spotted three girls, hurrying toward them. David took the snorkel out of his mouth and said, "It's Laura. She goes to my school."

"Come on," Luis mumbled, the snorkel still in his mouth. "Let's go." He backed farther into the ocean.

Carlos took the snorkel out of his mouth. "Which one is Laura?" he asked David.

"The blonde in the middle... with the ponytail."

Luis stopped, realizing his friends were delayed. He then joined them. Carlos and David took off their masks.

"Do you know the tall one with the black hair?" Carlos asked David.

"Her name is Silvia. She's a pain. They were both in my class."

"She looks older," Carlos observed, lowering his voice now that the girls were close by.

"That's because she has tits," Luis said out loud.

David pushed him, and Luis landed on his butt in the water.

"Hi, David," Laura said. Her smile showed a mouth full of braces. "You know Silvia, and this is our friend Marta." She pointed to the plump girl on her right.

"Who are your friends, David?" Silvia asked, staring into Carlos' green eyes. Marta moved away from Luis and moved next to Carlos.

"These are my best friends. This is Carlos," David said, noticing that Carlos was holding his stomach in and sticking out his chest. "And this is Luis." David noticed that the girls were ignoring Luis. Laura had not taken her eyes off David, and Silvia and Marta had their eyes glued to Carlos. David looked over Laura's shoulder and spotted her mother sitting on a towel nearby, keeping a close eye on them.

"Do you live in Miramar?" Silvia asked Carlos, throwing her chest forward. Her friend Marta just stood there staring at Carlos.

Luis stood by himself. David started to feel bad for him until Luis farted loudly.

"Excuse me," Luis said, deadpan. He put on his mask and snorkel and went underwater.

Carlos burst out laughing, then David joined in. The girls turned and walked away.

"Boys. They're so immature," David heard one of the girls complaining.

From Amigos to Friends

"Hey, Luis," Carlos yelled. "Wait for us."

Carlos and David dove after Luis, and skimming the surface of the crystal clear Caribbean waters, they swam toward the horizon. They slowly scanned the reef below, an exotic marine world ripe for exploration. Black sea urchins sat on red chunks of reef, jutting out as if reaching for the surface. Their long, slender thorns swayed rhythmically with the movement of the ocean's current. Schools of tiny, multicolored fish simultaneously darted in search of food and avoided becoming food for larger fish. Sand dollars were scattered along the reef, like loose change left behind. Bundles of seaweed grew out of sandy spots between the reef, their long, green blades slow-dancing to the ocean's rhythm. Tiny fish nibbled at minute marine organisms. A starfish stuck to the vertical surface of the reef, like the star on a theater dressing room door. A large school of silverfish, so big it cast a dark shadow on the ocean floor, passed nearby. Like a flock of birds in the sky, the school of fish turned simultaneously for no apparent reason. A group of four, no five... seven, eight palm-size squid floated three feet from the surface. Sensing danger, the squid contorted to a tube-like shape and propelled themselves a safe distance and depth from the three boys.

David inhaled hard through his snorkel, held his breath, and pursued the fleeing squid. Carlos and Luis dove after David. The squid fled deeper, propelling themselves farther and farther from the boys. Luis ran out of oxygen and headed up for air. He broke the surface, blew a column of water out of his snorkel, and took off his mask half-full with water. David came up on his right and Carlos on his left.

"Did you see that?!" David said, ripping the mask off his face. "Squid!"

David dove underwater. Carlos followed, then Luis. The water was warm and soothing, massaging their bodies as they glided through its liquid mass. On their backs, the strong Caribbean sun warmed their skin, and the sea provided ample light for the boys to see underwater, as if the water were clear glass. David saw it first and, with his heart pounding, dove down ten feet. He pointed at the three-inch, orange seahorse and motioned for Carlos and Luis to approach slowly. The tiny seahorse floated upright, holding onto a long, thin blade of seaweed with its tail twice coiled around the blade. As they circled the tiny creature, the boys' eyes darted from the seahorse to each other. Luis' hand reached to grab it. Carlos intercepted Luis' wrist inches from the delicate creature. Luis fought back, but was unable to shake loose from Carlos' grip. He then reached for the tiny seahorse with his other hand. David shoved the reaching hand away from the seahorse and ripped Luis' mask off his face. They struggled with each other as Luis went up for air. Breaking the surface first, Luis spit out a mouthful of water, choked, and took a deep breath through his mouth. Carlos and David surfaced and blew spouts of water out of their snorkels.

They spotted the breakwater seawall fifty feet away and swam to it. They pulled themselves up the two feet to the top of the seawall and, hacking and coughing, sat at the edge with their feet dangling in the ocean. Mischievously, David snatched Luis' mask.

"Give me my mask!" Luis ordered David angrily.

"You want your mask, Luis?" David asked, standing on the three-foot wide flat surface capping the seawall that fenced the cove and sheltered the small beach from crashing waves.

"Give it to me! Right now!"

Over Luis' head, David flipped the mask to Carlos. "I don't have your mask, Luis."

Carlos caught the mask and carefully shuffled farther back from Luis, trying not to slip on the wet green seaweed that carpeted the narrow ledge.

"You're going to pay for this," Luis promised him, inching closer to Carlos.

"Stop right there!" Carlos said. "... Or I'll throw your stuff in the water. On the other side!" Carlos' head gestured not to the side between the seawall and the beach, but the side where they had been warned, as far back as they could recall, never to swim.

Luis froze.

They knew stories of children swallowed by great white sharks, of giant octopuses wrapping their enormous tentacles around unsuspecting swimmers, dragging them down into deep underwater caves and sucking their blood with the huge suction cups in their tentacles, of barracudas who fed on the sex organs of teenage boys, of hammerhead sharks with three and four rows of six-inch-long, razor-sharp teeth.

"You don't have the guts," Luis said to Carlos, "because if you do, I'll throw you out there." His thumb pointed toward the horizon.

David slipped past Luis and planted himself between his friends. "Come on, you guys, cut it out," he said. "This is dangerous." David became frightened, recognizing the malicious grin suddenly appearing on Luis' face.

Luis jumped forward and shoved David into the water on the seaward side. Panic stricken, David screamed as he hit the water. Carlos heaved Luis' gear as far out to sea as he could, before realizing that his own mask and snorkel had gone with it. Luis grabbed him by the waist. They struggled. David screamed for help, trying to climb back onto the wall. He was almost back on top when Carlos and Luis, tangled up with each other, lost their balance and fell on top of David, dumping the three of them into the forbidden waters.

They trampled each other in the water, racing to reach the safety of the wall. They were pulling themselves up onto the seawall when Luis yelled, "Sharks!" and yanked Carlos and David back down into the ocean with him. Underwater, Luis grabbed his friends' bathing suits and dragged them down deep. They went under with Carlos and David thrashing, slugging and kicking Luis. When they finally broke the surface, gagging and coughing, they were ten feet away from the wall.

"I'm surprised we're still alive," Luis said, grinning.

David, who had held on to his mask, put it back on, and stuck his head underwater. He nervously surveyed their surroundings. He spotted a six-foot-long barracuda not more than ten feet away, calmly staring at them. David immediately protected his crotch with both hands, popped his head out of the water, and screamed, "BARRACUDA!"

Both Carlos and Luis instantly grabbed on to their genitals and stuck their heads underwater. The water was so clear that without masks they easily spotted the barracuda's shiny silhouette. They screamed underwater. The barracuda disappeared with a sudden motion. The boys's heads surfaced. They looked at each other and started laughing hysterically, holding on to their genitals, just in case.

On the third dive, they finally retrieved all their gear. Luis succeeded in daring them to stay out in the open ocean, until two passing fishermen in a rowboat warned them that they had recently spotted a couple of full-size hammerheads nearby.

To avoid being labeled cowards, all three swam slowly back to the breakwater, not wanting to be the first one back on the wall, but also not the last. They simultaneously climbed up onto the safety of the wall, their hearts pounding.

Luis left his feet dangling in the ocean and rested on his back on the hot, sun-baked seaweed carpeting the top of the breakwater.

"Wow, that was exciting," he said. "I wonder what it would be like to come face to face with a hammerhead?"

"You would have a heart attack, Luis," David said, taking off his fins. "That's what it would be like."

Carlos lay on his stomach at the edge of the wall, with his chin resting on his hands and his eyes fixed on the horizon.

From Amigos to Friends

"What do you think would be scarier?" he asked, "... to face a hammerhead in the ocean or a lion in the jungle?"

"Were you guys scared out there when we heard about the hammerheads?" Luis asked.

"Not really," Carlos said.

"Liar," David said.

"I was scared," Luis said. "But the more scared, the better."

"That's sick, Luis," David said.

Carlos jumped to his feet and pointed with his finger. "Look! Look!" he said. "Sharks!"

Luis jerked his feet out of the water and quickly stood up next to Carlos and David. In complete silence, for the longest time, their eyes followed two large, black fins slicing through the water not more than fifty feet from the wall.

When the fins finally disappeared from sight, the three of them turned and stared at each other. They shook. All color had drained from their faces. They just stood there. Carlos' mouth was open, a thin streak of saliva lining the side of his chin.

CHAPTER VII

A few weeks into that summer of 1961, David's father was driving back home from the store to meet the other parents. He replayed in his mind the encounter that morning that had triggered getting everyone immediately together. He concentrated, trying to recall every word and nuance, wanting to share every detail with the other parents.

It had been a slow morning at the store that day. The doorbell clanged and a well-dressed, middle-aged gentleman entered the store. David's father predicted that the customer would head for the book section. It was a guessing game he played to break up the monotony. The customer was too old to be a father, but too young to be a grandfather, so the toy section was not likely. The sports section seemed unlikely, too, given his slumped shoulders, ample waist, and awkward movements. The customer settled before a limited selection of philosophy books, giving Mr. Oviedo the satisfaction of being right.

He squinted and confirmed that the customer appeared familiar. The man extended his hand over the counter and introduced himself. He was the principal of David's private school and a renowned educator on the island.

"I had assumed you'd left the country," the educator said, "because David is no longer in school."

"No, no. With all the unrest," Mr. Oviedo said, "we decided it was best to keep him at home... since the school year was almost over anyway."

"You should leave for the United States," the man said, conclusively. "There's no future left in this country. Take your children out as soon as possible."

"What are you going to do?" Mr. Oviedo asked, hedging his bets.

"I'm leaving. I'm going to Miami," the educator said. "I'll have no part of brainwashing children with Communist propaganda."

"What are you talking about?"

"The government is going to close all private schools next year. The public schools already spend an hour a day indoctrinating children against religion and to embrace Communism."

"Are you positive? Are you sure?" Mr. Oviedo asked, alarmed.

"I attended a training session last week where they made a whole first-grade class close their eyes and pray to God for candy. When they were told to open their eyes, they found only disappointment. Then, they were told to close their eyes again and this time ask Fidel for candy. The teachers quietly distributed candy around the room so when the children opened their eyes, they found their wish fulfilled."

"Incredible!"

"I'm also aware of a program being implemented next year to immediately take children like your son to study in Russia, so when they finish college they will return home fully indoctrinated, as part of an elite group to run the country."

"They would take my son to Russia for all those years?"

"That's right."

"I wouldn't allow it!" David's father said firmly.

"Your son will soon no longer belong to you," the educator said with sadness in his eyes, "only to the Revolution."

Mr. Oviedo's '57 Dodge pulled into the driveway. David's father killed the engine and, closing his eyes, he rested his forehead against the steering wheel. The educator's words kept echoing in his head: "Your son will soon no longer belong to you, only to the Revolution."

An hour later, Carlos' parents and Luis' mother gathered at the Oviedo home. María had been given the afternoon off so they could talk freely. Mrs. Oviedo poured dark, strong Cuban coffee for the group.

"I didn't call your husband," Mr. Oviedo said to Mrs. Rodríguez, "because I didn't know how he would react to what we're going to talk about."

"You did the right thing. My husband is still acting blindly. It's better at this point if he's not aware of these conversations," she said, referring to the telephone calls Mr. Oviedo had made earlier that day to Carlos' parents and Luis' mother.

He briefly related to them what he had just heard from the educator.

"It's an absolute crime!" Mrs. Fernández said, pressing her fist against her left breast. "It gives me chest pains to even think that they would send my little boy to Russia. He would freeze to death."

"It's only a rumor, for all we know," Mr. Fernández said, dismissing his wife's comment.

"This man is a renowned educator," Mrs. Oviedo pointed out. "He's also a very responsible and serious man. I don't believe he would say it unless he had firsthand knowledge."

"What if it's not a rumor?" Mrs. Fernández said. "Are we going to take that chance?" She stood up and began pacing the room.

Mr. Fernández began pacing the room. "You're all getting hysterical over a rumor," he said. "Besides, Fidel isn't going to last."

"That's what you said two-and-a-half years ago when he took over the country," Mr. Oviedo reminded him.

"The Americans won't put up much longer with Communism ninety miles from their shores," he responded.

"Can't you see it's over," Mr. Oviedo argued back. "Kennedy didn't back the invasion. He's allowed it to exist. It's all over. Face reality!"

"If Castro fell from power, it would be even worse," Mrs. Rodríguez said.

All eyes turned to her, suspiciously. "What does that mean?" Mrs. Oviedo asked.

"If they take our boys away and Fidel falls, we'll never get our children out of Russia," she pointed out. "Read your history. It happened in Spain less than thirty years ago. After the Spanish Civil War, thousands of Spanish children who had been sent to Russia were kept in Russia."

"Oh, my God!" Carlos' mother said, collapsing back on the couch. "We would have to move to Russia."

"Stop talking nonsense!" her husband ordered, giving her a disapproving look.

"What are we going to do?" Mrs. Rodríguez asked. "What can we do?" She stopped pacing the room in front of David's parents and waited for their advice.

Mr. and Mrs. Oviedo turned toward their best friends and together said, "We're leaving. We're going to Miami."

The room was quiet. The silence was absolute.

"That's ridiculous," Mr. Fernández protested. "You're going to leave everything you've worked for all your life?" he said, gesturing around the expensively appointed living room. His gesture took in oil paintings, a marble sculpture adorning a corner, the bone china coffee set and the house itself to emphasize his point. "What about your professional careers? All for a stupid rumor?"

"You really mean it, don't you?" Mrs. Rodríguez said.

"We mean it," Mrs. Oviedo said. "We're leaving."

"We won't take the chance that it's only a rumor," Mr. Oviedo said. "But even if it is, there's no future left in our country for our children. We're willing to start all over again, if that's what it takes to guarantee them a worthwhile future."

"Well, thanks for making me look like a selfish bastard!" Mr. Fernández growled back.

"Be quiet," his wife said. "He didn't mean that!"

"Besides," Mr. Oviedo began, "they arrested me once. I was fortunate to get out alive. I don't think I'd survive a second time around."

Mrs. Fernández nodded.

"It may not be so easy for you to leave," Mr. Fernández pointed out. "I've heard the government is going to stop the exodus of professionals out of the country."

"We're willing to send David out first...until we can get out," Mr. Oviedo said. "His brother is too young. He'll have to wait with us."

"You're going to send your little boy to the United States all by himself?" Carlos' mother asked in shock.

"When I bought David the Mendoza boy's bicycle, his mother urged me to send David to Miami like she did with her son," Mr. Oviedo said. "I asked her the same question and she described a program in Miami set up by the Catholic Church that expedites American visas, and they take care of the children in the United States until the parents get out. She misses her son, but she feels good about how things have turned out. She called it the Peter Pan Project."

"What do they do with the children when they get to the United States?" Mrs. Fernández asked from the edge of her seat.

"They place them in foster homes or in private schools as interns."

"Oh God," Mrs. Fernández said, making the sign of the cross. "It sounds like we have no choice but to leave for the United States as soon as possible."

Mr. Fernández grabbed his wife's arm and made her get up. "You're all talking irrationally," he said. "I have to get back to the dealership." They reached the front door and said good-bye.

Pelayo "Pete" Garcia

Luis' mother followed them to the door. "It's going to be a long, hot summer," she predicted, closing the door behind her.

CHAPTER VIII

That summer, David, Carlos and Luis spent entire days at the beach. To break the monotony, but mostly to avoid Laura, Silvia and Marta, the boys made the rounds of all the clubs. Now that they were public clubs, membership was no longer an obstacle. The former Miramar Yacht Club remained their favorite. On stormy days, they would stretch out on top of the slippery surface of the breakwater and, gripping the edge of the wall with all their strength, they would be jolted as huge waves crashed against the breakwater. Once washed away, the challenge was to return to the wall before the next wave hit. Exhausted by the end of the day, with their feet peppered with sea urchin thorns, their hands missing chunks of flesh left behind on the wall's edge, they wearily returned to their homes. Their mothers would have fits at dinnertime, but David's and Carlos' fathers, who had "taken on the waves" themselves at the same spot as young men, would defuse their wives' objections. "As long as they don't go swimming on the other side of the wall, they're safe," the fathers would say. The boys nodded. Luis' father had missed out on such adventures, because by the time he was his son's age he had gone to work to help his father support his mother and eight younger brothers and sisters, but he enjoyed his son's escapades just the same and kept his wife off Luis' back.

The boys' second favorite place that summer was the public beach Luis had enjoyed with his family before the Revolution. It was called "The Bottle." In the past, the general public had been admitted by paying a small entrance fee. It was loud, the women wore skimpy bathing suits, and there was always a big band—trumpets, flutes, saxophones, guitars, congas, the works—playing *mambos, cha-cha, guarachas*. The Afro-Cuban beat provoked a sensuality that was frowned upon at the clubs, even now that they were public. It was not a place where Laura's mother would bring her daughter and her girlfriends. It was called "The Bottle" because the main attraction was a twenty-foot high concrete bottle sitting on a concrete platform perched on top of concrete pilings sticking ten feet out of the water, about a hundred feet from the shore. It was a gaudy scheme to advertise a cheap rum.

The boys became fascinated with the local practice of climbing the twenty slippery feet to the top of the bottle. The triumphant climber would stand up on its narrow top and then dive into the water thirty feet below. It had to be done headfirst, since it had been proven, time and time again, that jumping feet first would not clear the concrete platform below. For that matter, any slight slip while shoving off the top of the bottle would turn a headfirst dive into a concrete disaster. The injuries sustained in past mishaps were legendary, including three deaths. Luis took the plunge on their first visit and every day thereafter. Carlos jumped a week later, urged on by a beautiful mulatto girl. Finally, no longer able to handle the insinuations about his masculinity, David risked his life a week after Carlos. The whole experience had warranted a pact of secrecy.

An unexpected event, which in retrospect changed the course of that long summer, took place in mid-July while Carlos was off on his annual two-week summer stay at the farm that belonged to his mother's family. One afternoon when David and Luis returned home from a long day of skin-diving at the club, they found two motorcycles parked in Luis' driveway: his father's giant Harley and a 50cc grey Austrian-built Puch. They became hypnotized by the Puch. Luis fondled every inch of its black leather seat and shiny gun-barrel-grey chassis. David crouched on one knee, inspecting a chrome cylinder crowned by a Champion spark plug and fed by a multitude of wires and rubber hoses. On the polished chrome muffler, David spotted every freckle sprinkled across his cheeks and nose and noticed that his hair was turning auburn from all the sun and saltwater.

"You like it?" Luis asked.

"Of course, I like it," David said. "It's beautiful. I wonder how fast it can go."

"Sixty kilometers per hour," Luis announced, reading the speedometer. "It may be mine—I hope."

"Yours?"

"My father has been telling me he's going to buy me one as soon as he talks my mother into it," Luis said as he climbed on the motorcycle. His feet dangled, not quite touching the ground.

Luis' mother and father came out of the house and approached the motorcycle.

She planted her hands on her hips. "It's ridiculous," she said. "Look at that. His feet don't even reach the ground."

Luis stretched his legs and reached with his toes so that his tennis shoes scraped the driveway.

"He'll grow into it in a few months," Mr. Rodríguez said and proudly stood with his arm around his son's shoulders. "It's no faster than a three-speed bike."

Yeah, right! David thought.

Mrs. Rodríguez looked at her husband, suspiciously.

Understanding her body language, her husband answered her, "Paid for. With cash out of my salary."

"I guess it's all right," Mrs. Rodríguez said. "He's probably safer on his own than in back of that monster you ride." She pointed to the Harley.

Luis got off the motorcycle and began jumping up and down and hugging his parents.

Gee, I wish it would be that easy with my parents, David thought. His only consolation was that Luis' motorcycle had a back seat. It's going to be tough when Carlos returns next week and there are three of us. My chances of getting my own motorcycle are a zillion-to-one, he concluded, remembering how difficult it had been to talk his mother into a three-speed bicycle not so long ago.

"Come on, Luisito," Mr. Rodríguez said. "Let's go for a spin."

David's shoulders drooped and he turned to go home.

"Papi, can David ride behind me?" Luis asked.

Adrenaline flooded David's nervous system.

"No, Luisito," his father said. "Not until you've driven it for a few days and you get used to it."

David's spirits plunged into an abyss of despair. The solemn sadness reflected in his dark brown eyes must have touched Mr. Rodríguez, because he said, "Come on, David. You can ride with me."

David's heart skipped a beat as he climbed on the Harley behind Mr. Rodríguez.

After a brief set of instructions that Luis followed and David memorized, they took off. He was hooked the instant the wind hit his face. When he saw how good Luis looked riding alongside on his motorcycle, David made a personal vow that he would do whatever it took to get his own motorcycle as soon as possible.

The next morning, David ran three blocks down to the Shell station on Fifth Avenue and 98th Street to meet Luis. Luis was there adding a Coke bottle full of motor oil to the

Puch's tankful of gas. He stuck a wood stick in the tank and stirred.

"Why did you add oil to the gas tank?" David asked, climbing behind Luis.

"It's a two-stroke cylinder engine," Luis said with authority.

A block away from the gas station, they floored the engine and stared as the speedometer's needle plunged below the sixty kilometer-per-hour mark and stuck to the bottom of the dial. After much begging, Luis traded places with David. Confident that he had learned all there was to know by observing Luis that morning, David shifted into first gear, cranked the accelerator, and popped the clutch. The bike jumped forward. David gripped the handlebars. Luis clung to David's waist. The back tire burned rubber and the front wheel jumped up in the air and did not come back down to earth until twenty yards later.

"Hey!" Luis said, "let's do that again!"

They spent all morning speeding everywhere they felt safe that their parents would not find out. At lunchtime, they stopped at the club. At the counter, they endured single-slice ham sandwiches on white bread and glasses of water with no ice. The ice machine and the toaster had been broken for several weeks. Ham sandwiches would not have been their first choice, since they mostly consisted of fat, but it was today's special—meaning it was the only thing available.

"Hey, Luis," David said, "have you noticed a change in your parents' behavior lately?"

Luis bit into his sandwich and shrugged his shoulders. "What do you mean?"

"Aren't they more lenient? Easier on the rules?"

"I don't know," Luis said, "my father hasn't changed a bit."

"I'll give you an example," David said. "Aren't you surprised how easily your mother agreed to let you have a motorcycle."

"I guess so," Luis said. "Now that I think about it, my mother is more lenient."

"I went home last night and at dinner I told my parents that your parents had given you a motorcycle," David said. "My plan was to beg them for permission to ride with you. I never even considered asking to be allowed to drive it. And I thought getting one of my own was at least two years into the future, if ever."

"And what happened?" Luis asked.

"My father asked me if I wanted one," David said. "And my mother didn't even put up a fight."

"Do you think you'll get one?" Luis asked, excitedly.

"I'm positive," David said. "I'm telling you, Luis. Something weird is going on."

Just as David had predicted, two days after his conversation with Luis, while David was eating breakfast with his family, his dream became a reality.

"We have a surprise for you," Mr. Oviedo said.

"For both of you," his mother added.

Mr. Oviedo led his sons to the garage. First, David spotted his brother's brand new Russian-made, military-green tricycle with oversized back wheels. He gasped when he then spotted next to his mother's grey Oldsmobile Delta 88, a fire-engine red, 50cc Puch motorcycle. It was the same size engine as Luis', but it was the deluxe model with the gas tank extending from the steering wheel to the seat, just like the ones on the big motorcycles.

David slowly approached the motorcycle and memorized every detail: the shiny, waxed chassis, the black-as-ink tires, the gleaming chromed engine and muffler, the black leather seat with only a few scratches. He mounted the bike, feeling like a king sitting on his throne.

From Amigos to Friends

He checked the big, round speedometer—sixty kilometers per hour! It gave him goose bumps. I wonder how fast I can make it go after I strip it down, he wondered.

"It's used, but not much," Mr. Oviedo pointed out, breaking David's reverie. "It only has three thousand kilometers on the odometer."

David checked—two thousand nine hundred eighty-seven to be exact. David gripped the handlebars and worked the clutch and the three speeds, all on the left side, then the front brake on the right side and the back brakes on the pedals.

"Go ahead. Crank it up," his father said.

David opened a valve, transferring fuel from the gas tank to the carburetor, checked to see that it was in neutral, set the pedals in place, and in one swift motion he jumped on the pedal. The engine came alive. David revved it up several times, filling the garage with exhaust fumes. Mr. Oviedo rushed to open the garage door to let out the carbon monoxide and replace it with fresh air. David's brother pedaled his tricycle out onto the driveway. His mother followed closely behind, leaving David alone with his father.

"I love you, son. Please be careful with it. Your mother and I will die if you get hurt."

"I love you too, Papi," David said, feeling his father shaking. "I'll be careful. I promise."

Mr. Oviedo's eyes held his son's. "I want you to go outside and thank your mother. She's not crazy about this. She's sure you're going to get hurt."

"Why then are you and Mami giving me this motorcycle?"

Mr. Oviedo looked away. "Don't you want it?"

"I want it. It's beautiful, but..."

"The classified ad in the paper read: 'If you see it, you'll buy it!' I saw it and I bought it for you," Mr. Oviedo said. "I think you're old enough and mature enough if you control your fascination with speed and you don't let those two wild friends of yours talk you into doing things you know you shouldn't do." Mr. Oviedo hugged his son. "Now go out there and promise your mother."

"Wow! Look at that!" Luis yelled, approaching the garage.

David climbed on the Puch and fired up the engine.

Luis slowly walked around his friend's bike, whistling in admiration. "Is it new?" he asked.

"Almost," Mr. Oviedo said, proudly. "Son, kill the engine before we asphyxiate!"

"Let's go take it for a spin instead," Luis said and climbed behind David.

David began to move the motorcycle forward when his father's eyes stopped him. David killed the engine and said to Luis, "I have to go thank my mother. It may take a few minutes."

━·━·━

David and Luis spent the week before Carlos' return planning the most dramatic and cruel way to use their new motorcycles to devastate Carlos upon his return. Carlos had always been the one to have things first. Carlos had the first radio, the first high-fidelity record player, the first three-speed bike and the first Mickey Mantle baseball card. He had also been the first one to see a major league baseball game, when his father took him along on a business trip to Detroit. At Tiger stadium, they saw the Yankees beat the Detroit Tigers 5-to-2 when Mickey Mantle, with a three-and-two count and the bases loaded in the ninth inning, hit one over the left-field fence. Carlos returned from the trip with a Yankees' cap on his head and a Raleigh baseball in his hand. "This is the home run ball Mickey Mantle hit," he bragged. "I caught it with my bare hand!" He would leap up in the air and catch an imaginary ball with his left arm stretched out so far that it looked like his arm was about to come out of its socket. When Luis and David asked why Carlos had not brought back two extra baseball caps for his best friends, Carlos innocently said,

From Amigos to Friends

"How did I know you guys would want one?" That conversation ended in a fistfight with Luis holding Carlos down and David punching away. Carlos' lie about the home run ball was confirmed one day when his father made a comment about how disappointing it had been to watch the Yankees lose and not even get to see Mantle get on base. David and Luis sentenced Carlos to the "silent treatment" for a whole week.

The time had arrived to get even. It was a vicious plan, but Carlos deserved it. Deciding that the motorcycles alone were not enough torture, David and Luis formed a motorcycle club; of course, membership was limited to motorcycle owners. Realizing the advantage of doctoring the engines to make them faster without their parents' suspicious eyes constantly upon them, they decided to house the club ten blocks away at Carlos' grandmother's house. The old mansion had been built when a household required a multitude of servants who were housed in quarters above a detached two-car garage. The garage area was perfect to work on the bikes, and the now empty upstairs became the club's headquarters. Luis and David decorated the walls of the room, which contained only a dilapidated, brown couch, with bright motorcycle-racing-scenes posters they had found when they scoured the city for spare parts, after learning that the Puch dealership was going out of business. The company had long ago stopped importing to the island.

They confirmed the date of Carlos' return when they inadvertently stumbled into Mr. Fernández. David and Luis had left Luis' house very early that morning—a few minutes after five to be exact—not to go fishing as they had lied to their parents, but to ride their motorcycles to Guanabacoa, a nearby town where they had heard a mechanic had a shop full of motorcycle spare parts for sale. They had decided to leave before dawn to minimize the chances of getting caught going on a trip that their parents would never allow. They were right in front of Carlos' house when Mr. Fernández's Cadillac turned the corner. The boys quickly attempted to hide, but were suddenly trapped by Mr. Fernández's headlights. The car pulled into the driveway, and Carlos' father pulled them over.

"When did you get those motorcycles?" he asked, getting out of the Cadillac.

"Last week," David said, noticing that Mr. Fernández's clothes were very wrinkled.

Mr. Fernández noticed David looking at his clothes and said, checking his watch, "My, it's late. I had so much work at the dealership I had to pull an all-nighter."

"We want to surprise Carlos," Luis said. "Please don't tell him about the motorcycles."

"Hey, I understand," he said, conspiratorially. "It'll be our secret. We never ran into each other."

"When is Carlos coming back?" David asked and noticed that Mr. Fernández was missing a sock.

"Monday morning," he replied, heading toward his front door.

Very early on Monday morning, David and Luis quietly pushed their motorcycles onto Carlos' property and hid them out of sight from both Carlos' balcony and his front door. They cautiously surveyed the surroundings to make sure Rocky was not lurking around and then headed for the front door. "Stop snickering," David whispered. Luis knocked.

"Hi, guys!" Carlos said, opening the door wearing a white cowboy hat, a black western shirt, jeans, and cowboy boots. He held a photograph in his hand.

"Hi, Carlos," David and Luis said, realizing that Carlos was up to something, but confident that this time he was completely out-gunned.

Carlos handed his friends the photograph. "That's Snow, my new horse. My mother bought him for me. He's the best. I broke him in myself."

David and Luis glanced at a photo of Carlos on a beautiful white horse, clad in the same white cowboy hat and outfit he now wore.

"That's great, Carlos," David said, yawning, and handing Carlos back the photograph.

Carlos, disappointed with his friends' lack of envy, stepped up his plan. "Look what else I got," he said. He disappeared for a second and returned with a skin-diver's spear. "You guys don't have to worry anymore about hammerheads with me carrying this baby around. Well? Are we going diving, or what?" His face was full of teeth, his chest puffed out, his stomach sucked in.

"No, we don't do that kind of stuff anymore," David said.

"It's too immature," Luis added.

Carlos' teeth disappeared, and his stomach and chest traded sizes. "What do you mean?"

"We're into motorcycles now, Carlos," David said, feigning a yawn.

"Motorcycles?" Carlos asked.

"Yeah, David and I spend the day driving motorcycles, or at the motorcycle club," Luis said, shoving the knife in deeper.

"Motorcycle club?" Carlos said. "Whose motorcycle club are you talking about?" Carlos asked, now expecting the worst.

"Luis' and mine," David said.

"Are you saying you two have your own motorcycles?" Carlos asked, hoping he was only having a nightmare.

"Yeah," David said. "Do you want to see them?"

"Okay," Carlos said, resentfully.

Luis led the way. "You can look, but don't touch. Okay, Carlos?" David said, leading the sheep to the slaughter.

After a long day stuck alternating riding behind David and Luis, but not being allowed to drive, and seeing the motorcycle club, but not being allowed to apply for membership because he did not own a motorcycle, Carlos went home so upset that he woke up in the middle of the night burning with fever. When his mother read the thermometer and told her son she was going to call the doctor, Carlos assured her that the only thing that would save his life was a motorcycle. Then he went on to question his parents' love for him. He pointed out that his parents must not have the same affection for him as David's and Luis' parents had for their sons. His mother spent the rest of the night arguing that his accusation was unfair and groundless. Carlos questioned how she could ignore the fact that he was the only one in the neighborhood without a motorcycle. His mother pointed out that David and Luis were not the only boys in the neighborhood. Carlos argued that he, David, and Luis were the only ones that counted, and when it was convenient for his mother, like when she lectured him about getting better grades, she always brought David up and nobody else. In tears, his mother told him that she was deeply hurt by his accusations. He pointed out that he was not accusing her of not loving him, but only making an observation. After Mrs. Fernández promised her son that she would do her best to talk her husband into buying Carlos a motorcycle, Carlos mentioned that he already felt a little better and then described to his mother in great detail, the brand, model, and color he wanted.

The next morning, the family doctor made a house call and concluded that Carlos had the flu and would return to one hundred percent in a few days. After the doctor's departure, Mrs. Fernández returned to her son's side and gave him the good news that his father had agreed to buy him a motorcycle. Carlos ran to the phone and alerted David and Luis to immediately start searching for the bike of his dreams. Since money was no object when Carlos' health was on the line, David and

Luis set out on their quest, confident that they would succeed, their pockets stuffed with Mrs. Fernández's money.

On the first day, they tracked down a 50cc, fire-engine red, Italian-built Victoria Avanti beauty. The money changed hands and after chaining David's motorcycle to a light pole, they raced to Carlos' house. The seller had volunteered to deliver it, but the boys decided to avoid the risk of the man changing his mind. David and Luis had by now satisfied their need to make Carlos suffer and were tired of dragging him around town behind them.

Announcing their arrival by blasting their horns from a block away, they arrived at Carlos' house by mid-afternoon. Carlos came out on the balcony in his pajamas and started jumping up and down when he spotted the Victoria Avanti. Mrs. Fernández came out on the balcony and tried to calm him down. Seconds later, Carlos ran out of the house barefoot. Mrs. Fernández trailed behind, pleading for her son to step into a pair of bedroom slippers and to put on a sweater she brought with her.

After reluctantly indulging his mother, Carlos reached his bike with the slippers and the sweater on, despite the scorching summer sun. David dismounted and Carlos climbed on, his face flushed with heat and excitement.

"Carlitos, get off that motorcycle and get back in bed," Mrs. Fernández pleaded with her son. "You're sick."

Carlos fired up the engine. "Mami, I'm just going around the block. I'll be right back."

His mother stepped in front of the motorcycle to block his way. "Carlitos, you're sick. You're weak and you've never driven one before."

"Mami, I feel fine. I know what I'm doing."

His mother felt his forehead. "You're burning up," she said.

Carlos pushed the bike forward. His mother moved in self-defense. "Just around the corner, please!"

"Carlitos, you're impossible," Mrs. Fernández said, planting her hands on her hips. "Go ahead, but don't forget what your father said this morning. If you get hurt... even a scratch... we immediately sell the motorcycle."

Carlos nodded and took off. Mrs. Fernández stormed into the house. David and Luis, knowing that Carlos had never driven a motorcycle before, ran after him.

Carlos reached the corner in four wide zigzags, hit the curb when he overshot the intersection, flew over the handlebars, and landed in a neighbor's yard. When they reached Carlos, they found him crying and nursing his left arm.

"I think I broke my arm!" he announced. His face was masked with pain.

"Oh no!" David said. "Now they're going to sell your bike."

Luis picked up the bike and killed the engine.

"Is it okay?" Carlos asked Luis.

"Not a scratch," Luis said.

"Good! good!" Carlos said in tears.

"What are you going to do?" David asked, helping Carlos up.

"I won't tell them," Carlos said, finding his slippers and putting them on. Pain shot up and down his arm.

"But your arm is broken!" Luis pointed out.

"Help me get home," Carlos said. "In a couple of days, I'll tell them that I broke it playing baseball."

"You're crazy," David said.

"Doesn't it hurt a lot?" Luis asked.

"Yes, but it would hurt more to lose my motorcycle."

David and Luis agreed with Carlos' logic and helped him to his bed.

In the middle of the night, no longer able to withstand the excruciating pain, Carlos screamed. His parents found him in a heap at the bottom of the stairs.

From Amigos to Friends

A half-hour later, Mrs. Fernández explained to the emergency room doctor how her son had tripped in the dark and fallen down the stairs while going to get a drink of water.

CHAPTER IX

During the following six weeks—the four weeks in August and the first two weeks in September—Carlos wore a cast on his left arm. The cast did not interfere with his ability to drive his precious Victoria Avanti motorcycle or play the guitar, but it did keep him from joining David and Luis underwater.

On the days the boys went to the club, David and Luis would "catch waves" if the surf was up, or go snorkeling otherwise. Carlos would join them as far as the shore, and then he would practice his guitar under the shade of a coconut tree. And like clockwork, within minutes, Laura, Marta, and Silvia flocked to his feet.

At first, David and Luis laughed when Carlos told painful stories about having to talk to the girls and enduring their weird conversations. He swore that he would give anything to be able to dive underwater and disappear from their sight. He would scream at the cast as if it were solely to blame.

But as time passed, David and Luis noticed that Carlos stopped complaining quite as much. And from a distance, they observed that he appeared to enjoy himself when surrounded by the three girls and occasionally even Laura's mother. David and Luis always joined the group when Laura's mother sat with them. She had a beautiful face and a spectacular figure, with a pair of breasts that made David and Luis overlook the girls' silliness.

Their suspicion that Carlos was secretly enjoying himself with the girls became irrefutable one hot Tuesday morning in early September. Coming out of the water after a long diving stretch, David and Luis flopped down on the sand next to Carlos, who was playing the guitar under the coconut tree. The three girls sat admiringly at his feet. Carlos finished the song, and the girls clapped and sighed simultaneously.

"David, I'm having a birthday party Saturday afternoon," Laura said. "Would you come?"

David's breathing stopped. He would've rather heard that his hair was on fire than to have Laura ask him to go to a party in front of his friends.

"It's going to be a lot of fun," Marta said to Luis, who had begun attracting her attention ever since the day he showed up on his motorcycle. "You can be my dance partner."

"Dancing?" Luis asked. His forehead turned into a raisin. "I don't dance," he said, as if denying committing a mass murder.

David noticed that Carlos' face was as red as Silvia's lipstick. Then Silvia's words confirmed their worst suspicions: "Carlos is coming to the party with me," she said possessively. She pulled her hair behind her right ear and draped it over her right breast. "Carlos promised."

Luis' jaw dropped. David searched Carlos' eyes, hoping for a denial, but Carlos looked away.

"It's my fourteenth birthday," Laura said to David. "Next year will be the big party. It'll be my fifteenth, my coming-out-into-society party." Her face flushed with anticipation.

"There's going to be chocolate cake and ice cream," the traitor said, trying to melt his friends' ice-cold stares, "and I'm bringing my Elvis Presley record collection."

David's eyes shifted back and forth from Laura to Luis. She smiled and he frowned. David felt torn. He wanted to say yes. He wanted to go to Laura's birthday party on Saturday. He wanted to wear the new loafers with metal taps he had never worn, the new navy blue pants and yellow button-down shirt his mother had bought for him. With Laura in his arms, he wanted to try out the dance steps he had practiced by himself in front of the mirror. And mostly, he wanted to touch Laura, to hold her in his arms and to press his body against hers while they danced, as he had seen done on television and at the movies.

Luis broke the long silence. "I can't go," he said. "David and I made plans to go to the television station with my father," he lied and gave David a look that said, you owe me one. I just saved you from a fate worse than doing homework.

David stared into Laura's eyes and read her disappointment. Her whole face turned sad. "Luis," David said, "I thought it was next weekend when we're supposed to go out with your father."

Laura's face brightened, but Luis' turned into a scowl.

"Yeah, Luis," Carlos quickly jumped in. "I was there. I heard your father. David is right. You have your weekends mixed-up."

Luis raised his voice. "You're the one who's all mixed-up, Carlos," Luis said and stomped away.

"I'll let you know tomorrow," he said to Laura and quickly went after Luis. Carlos reluctantly left the girls and followed his male friends.

Luis refused to recognize his friends' presence, the whole way to the locker room. Luis reached his locker and flopped down on the wood bench. David sat next to him. Carlos sat next to David.

"What are you so mad about?" Carlos asked, sarcastically. "It's just a party."

"Luis, it's only for a couple of hours. We'll listen to some music. We'll have cake and ice cream, and then we'll leave," David said, sympathetically.

Luis' silence kept Carlos and David talking.

"We have nothing to do this Saturday anyway," Carlos pointed out.

"Yeah, Luis," David agreed, "it's not like we have anything planned and we're bailing out on you. We want you to come with us."

"That's right," Carlos agreed.

Luis stared at both of them with a blank expression worthy of a veteran poker player.

"Look, Luis," David offered. "If you don't want to go, we won't go. Right, Carlos?" David kept waiting for Carlos' agreement to come over his shoulder. After a very long wait, David finally glanced over his shoulder and, when he read Carlos' face, he realized he was in the middle of a three-way friendship crisis.

"Okay," Luis said, "let's not go."

"Fine," David said, reluctantly, "we won't go." He turned around to face Carlos.

"We can either go to the television station with my father or we can go to the movies... to the matinee," Luis said.

"Sounds good to me," David lied, soliciting Carlos' comments, but not receiving any feedback. Great, David thought, now he won't talk.

"It's settled then," Luis said, getting up, "we'll go to the movies."

"The hell with you, Luis," Carlos said, squaring off with Luis. "I don't want to go to the movies. I want to go to the party."

David moved between Carlos and Luis. "I have an idea," David said. "Why don't we go to the party for a while and then to the movies?"

"That's okay with me," Carlos said, controlling his temper.

"I won't go to a stupid party," Luis said. "I'm not going to get all dressed up and act like an idiot, like Carlos does around those ugly girls."

"Wait a minute, Luis," David said, defending Laura. "They're not all ugly."

"The one that likes Luis is the only ugly one," Carlos said, "and she only likes him because he has a motorcycle."

Luis threw a jab over David's shoulder that landed on Carlos' chin, sending him crashing against the wooden lockers. David held Luis back. Carlos jumped over the bench, and over David's shoulder grabbed Luis' head. All three ended up on the concrete floor, with Carlos and Luis trying to hurt each other and David trying to separate them.

The locker-room attendant finally split them apart and forced them to shake hands, "like gentlemen." David took advantage of the short conciliation to strike a deal. Carlos took back what he had said in exchange for Luis attending the party. Luis agreed to go to the party on two conditions: that he wouldn't be stuck with Marta, and that they would stay no longer than two hours.

Early Saturday morning, Luis arrived at David's house and announced he had a terrible stomachache. "I can't go to the party after all," were the first words out of his mouth.

David took Luis directly to his mother. Dr. Oviedo poked Luis' stomach, checked inside his mouth and gave him two heaping tablespoons of medicine, while Luis protested, claiming that the pain had suddenly disappeared.

Drenched in sweat from the summer heat and the long-sleeved shirt he wore, Carlos arrived a few minutes later. He had been to the doctor the night before and had had the cast removed in time for the party. The long-sleeved shirt and Carlos' unusually subdued behavior confirmed to David and Luis that Carlos had something up his sleeve. Carlos' lack of candor left his friends with no choice but to rip the sleeves of the shirt. To their amazement, they found that one arm appeared normal, but the one that had been in the cast for the last six weeks looked as if it had spent the entire summer in a darkroom. Camouflaging his threat as friendly advice, Luis suggested that Carlos skip the party, unless he wanted to become the laughingstock of everyone, especially the girls. David tempered Carlos' mood by simply lying: "It doesn't look that bad. And nobody will notice under a long-sleeved shirt." Unless Luis told, of course. Although Carlos hounded Luis to promise not to tell, Luis remained uncommitted.

Back at his house, Carlos inhaled lunch and rushed upstairs to get ready for the party. In his room, he sat on the floor in front of a three-foot high pile of long-playing records. He carefully evaluated each one, forming two piles. When he finished, he realized he had selected enough music, not for two hours, but for two days and reluctantly thinned out the "yes" pile. He rifled through his closet and laid out several shirt-sand slack combinations on the bed. In front of the mirror, he stripped down to his Jockey shorts. He sucked in his stomach, heaved his chest, raised his arms, and flexed his biceps. Nothing happened. Frustrated, he hit the floor and did ten pushups, cheating on the last five. He turned over and struggled through twenty sit-ups. He tried the mirror again and, frustrated, decided to get dressed. Zipping up his pants, he wondered, as he often did, what Silvia looked like naked. He began undressing her in his mind, while buttoning his long-sleeved shirt. He hadn't kissed Silvia at the beach, but was certain that he could have if her girlfriends had not been around.

Brushing his teeth while carefully checking in the mirror to make sure no black beans from lunch lingered between his teeth, he made up his mind to kiss Silvia on the lips. The first kiss of his life. He closed his eyes and in his mind's eye, he practiced—just like Rock Hudson did it in the movies. After twenty minutes of fussing with his hair which was a shiny blonde from a whole summer in the sun, he grabbed his long-playing and 45 RPM records, and headed to meet his friends at David's house.

From Amigos to Friends

Immobilized, Luis sat on his bed, wondering how to act at Laura's party. He had no clue. He considered using his parents as role models, but discarded the thought, recalling only anger and disagreements. He considered using humor, but concluded his brand was too dark and over the girls' heads. What am I going to do? he asked himself. Who am I when I go to this party?

He went to the phone and dialed his father's apartment, but there was no answer. He called the television station and, after a long time on hold, he was told his father was too busy to come to the phone and would call him back tomorrow. He slammed the phone down. He looked up and found his mother waiting to help. She told him that he was handsome enough and that girls want more than looks alone. "Tell them some of the stories you've written," Mrs. Rodríguez suggested. "It was your father's love letters that I fell in love with." She told him that he would not be the only one nervous, that girls get nervous too—they just hide it better. "Be a gentleman," she said. "Girls like boys who have good manners." When she asked him why he had laughed when she had mentioned being well behaved and sensitive, he didn't dare tell his mother about the farting incident.

Thanks to his mother's support, he felt more confident and finished dressing. He stopped to say good-bye and found his mother hunched over her sewing machine. He didn't have an explanation for why he had dressed all in black. He argued with her, telling her he would stay home if he had to wear anything else. She relented, gave him a kiss, and told him to just be himself and have fun.

Wondering why he had, in fact, chosen to dress all in black and why he had decided to skip the deodorant and brushing his teeth, Luis started for David's house.

Pelayo "Pete" Garcia

Impatiently tapping his foot, David stood in front of María while the maid meticulously ironed his new yellow, button-down shirt. He had tried it on that morning, as in a dress rehearsal, and had found it too stiff. María had then hand-washed it and was now ironing it to his specifications. He told her to deliver it to his bedroom when it was perfect and went to take a shower. He had never taken a shower without waiting the required digestion time, but then again, he had never gone to a party at the invitation of a girl. With his parents at the store, he decided to stay in the shower as long as he wanted. He hated how his mother always yelled at him to get out of the shower and "stop wasting water."

Stepping into the shower, he remembered his father telling him about going out to dinner that evening without his brother. Why Saturday and not Sunday, when we usually go out to dinner on María's day off, he wondered. Why only the three of us? They always took his little brother along every-where. I wonder what's going on, he thought. I wonder if maybe we're moving to the United States, like so many other families from Miramar. Maybe tonight I'll find out what's going on.

He stuck his head under a torrential flow of hot water, and his thoughts melted back to Laura.

He wondered if she would like what he was going to wear. He was glad he had insisted on having María wash the shirt. It had been too stiff and he wanted Laura to feel good in his arms. He was glad that his mother had convinced him to take Laura a gift, even though Laura's mother had said not to bring presents. "I know how hard it is to find anything to buy these days," she had said. He was proud of the tortoise-shell hair clip he was giving Laura. He was sure she would like it and would wear it on her ponytail the minute she opened the gift. He felt bad that his mother had to part with her hair clip, but she made it easy when she said that she never used it and that there was nothing at the stores worth buying these days. He sensed that he was running late and started washing his hair.

━━━━━

David rang the doorbell, firmly holding Laura's gift in his other hand. Carlos stood behind him, loaded down with records and wearing too much cologne. Luis stood out in the sun feeling perspiration trickling under his armpits. He suspected it would soon turn into body odor, and half-moons would appear under each arm. Carlos made a disparaging remark about the Cuban music filtering out of the house.

David was reprimanding Carlos with a dirty look for his unacceptable behavior, when Laura's mother answered the front door. She complimented them on how handsome they looked and asked them inside. Then she spotted Luis out in the yard burning up in the sun. She recognized him as the seamstress's son and hesitated to let him in her house, but she felt sorry for him, melting away under the blazing summer sun, dressed all in black. She asked him to come inside.

Carlos carried his record collection directly to the record player and proclaimed himself the official disc jockey.

Blushing, Laura went to David. Dragging his loafers as noisily as possible, David met her in the middle of the spacious living room. Their eyes locked. David's mind went blank. Instead of the clever line he had composed and practiced all morning, he simply said, "Happy birthday." He handed Laura the little package that his mother had wrapped so beautifully.

She held the gift without saying a word. Marta and Silvia reached their side.

Dragging Luis behind her, Laura's mother broke in. She took the gift from her daughter. "You'll open it later," she said. "Now let's go out to the back yard and get this party going."

David was disappointed. He wanted Laura to wear the hair clip on her long, blond ponytail. Luis checked his watch.

An hour and fifty-six minutes to go, he calculated. Carlos carefully set the needle down, and Elvis started singing "My Puppy Love."

In the back yard, several dozen kids, some from the neighborhood and others from school, were gathered among the multicolored balloons decorating the entire back yard and porch. Against a wall was a long table full of finger sandwiches, pastries, cookies, and a four-decker chocolate-frosted cake as the centerpiece. Two maids in white uniforms swatted flies away from the food.

The party consisted of three groups: the boys on one side, giggling teenage girls across the yard from the boys, and parents gossiping in the shade.

The girls wore pastel dresses, ribbons in their hair, summer sandals on their feet, pearl or diamond earrings on their ears, and fresh, excited smiles on their faces. The boys, except Luis, wore brightly colored polo shirts, cotton slacks, and loafers with white socks, but no smiles.

Laura's mother led her daughter, two girlfriends, Carlos, David and Luis to the middle of the dance floor. She asked for dance volunteers to break the ice. Luis fled as if a fire alarm had gone off. David excused himself to go to the bathroom. Carlos ran to turn the volume up. The three girls started rock-and-rolling with each other.

With forty-two minutes left to go, Luis finished his third plate of cake and ice cream and plotted how to dip his glass in the rum punch one of the maids was serving the adults. Carlos slow-danced so close to Silvia that several parents registered their complaints with Laura's mother.

David and Laura gossiped about other kids at the party until, with twenty-one minutes to go, Laura finally talked David onto the dance floor. It was a slow tune, the Spanish version of an American song about a boy pleading with Venus, the goddess of love, to find him a girl to fall in love with. David held her firmly in his arms, felt her warm cheek against his face, and then the rest of her soft curvaceous body pressed against his. He panicked when he felt his pants bulging and discreetly pulled back from her. She moved closer to him and closed her eyes. He again panicked when the song ended and a fast one began.

With only twelve minutes and thirty-five seconds left, Carlos and Luis struck a deal. An hour-and-a-half extension, if Carlos succeeded in helping Luis get to the rum punch, or better yet, to the source itself: the bottle of Bacardi rum.

An hour and twelve minutes into the overtime period, thanks to three filled-to-the-rim glasses of rum punch, Luis asked Marta to dance. The party had thinned down to the three couples: Carlos and Silvia, David and Laura, Luis and Marta. They were wilted from the heat and the vigorous dancing to Carlos' rock-and-roll collection. Luis moved with exaggerated motions, his eyes closed. In the background, the maids cleaned up the empty plates and glasses left behind, took down the balloons, and rearranged the back yard furniture to normal. A slow tune began, Elvis' "Love Me Tender." Laura's mother left the patio and the three couples began to slow dance. Carlos and Silvia started kissing on the mouth. The other four stared at them. Silvia's eyes were closed. Carlos' eyes were open, witnessing his own experience as if registering every detail for posterity. David and Laura vacillated. Their lips were about to touch when they heard Luis' voice say loudly, "You better not kiss me, Marta. I have really bad breath."

David and Laura started laughing. She hid her face in David's shoulder, and then her big green eyes, full of mischief, held his. Her lips were moist and slightly parted. Her body stuck to his. Her heart pounded against his chest. He closed his eyes and their lips were about to touch when they heard her mother say, "Laura, it's time for these boys to go home."

In a fraction of a second, David and Laura stood three feet apart, their virgin lips intact, their faces as red as Laura's dress. Carlos and Silvia kept dancing, glued to each other. Luis asked Laura's mother if he could have something to drink. He offered to settle for some punch, if nothing else was available. Laura's mother stormed into the house. The music ended with the sound of the needle scratching through the record. Alarmed, Carlos jumped out of Silvia's arms and ran inside the house.

Holding onto the front door, Laura's mother impatiently waited for the boys to leave. Disappointed, the girls remained behind in the living room. Luis stumbled out onto the porch and zigzagged through the manicured front yard and then onto the sidewalk. Carlos, loaded down with his pile of precious records, passed Laura's mother and gave her a dirty look. She smiled back.

David stopped at the threshold, turned around and said to Laura, "I hope you like the gift. Happy birthday."

Laura pleaded with her mother to let her open the gift in front of David. She refused.

David turned to Laura's mother. "Thank you very much for inviting me to the party," David said. "You have a beautiful home and I had a wonderful time. Thank you again."

Laura's mother cracked a smile, and David walked out.

Reaching their motorcycles, Carlos and David agreed that Luis shouldn't drive. Luis started to argue that he was perfectly sober, when he tripped over his own foot, fell down on the grass, and threw up. David strapped Luis to his back and then he and Carlos left on their motorcycles.

They ended up at the motorcycle club where Luis passed out on the old brown couch. Carlos and David sat on the floor with their backs against the front of the couch.

"Did you kiss her?" Carlos asked.

"I almost did," David answered.

"I kissed Silvia," Carlos said with a proud smile. "Did you see me?"

"I saw you. And so did the whole world," David said, "including Laura's mother."

"That witch," Carlos said, his smile turning into a frown. "I can't believe she ruined my record. She did it on purpose."

"How did it feel?" David asked.

"It felt terrible," Carlos quickly said, "like a knife cutting through my stomach!"

Confused, David stared at his friend. Carlos stared back. Simultaneously, they realized they were talking about different things and started laughing.

"It was great," Carlos said and licked his upper lip.

"What did it feel like?"

"Wet... soft... I don't know. I wasn't thinking about it," Carlos said. "She's experienced. She gave me her tongue right away."

"She did not!" David said, challenging Carlos.

"It was a real turn-on," Carlos admitted. "I wasn't sure I would like it. You know when you stop and think about it, it doesn't sound too good."

"I've always thought the same thing," David admitted.

"I once asked my father if people really used their tongues when they kissed," Carlos said. "He said yes and then told me not to look so worried, because I would end up liking it a lot."

"I wonder if Laura has ever kissed another guy?" David said.

"Hey," Carlos said, "who would you rather kiss, Marilyn Monroe or Sophia Loren?"

"Marilyn Monroe," David quickly answered.

"No way," Carlos said. "Sophia has bigger breasts."

"You said kiss," David said. "You didn't say anything about touching. Besides, I like blondes better."

"Okay," Carlos said. "Whose breasts would you rather feel. Marilyn Monroe's or Sophia Loren's?"

"Hey, Carlos," David said. "Did you..."

"No, I tried, but she kept blocking me," Carlos said.

David suddenly checked his watch and jumped to his feet. "I have to run," he said. "I was supposed to be home ten minutes ago. I'm going out to dinner with my parents." He ran out of the room.

On the five-minute ride home, David's thoughts outran his motorcycle. Life was great. Every day was exciting. There wasn't a thing he would change.

CHAPTER X

Surprised and yet relieved that his parents had not reprimanded him for being late, David sat in the back seat of his father's car. In between his mother's questions about the party and his monosyllabic answers, David wanted to savor every detail, every moment he had experienced that afternoon at Laura's party. Closing his eyes and pressing his hand against his cheek, he sensed her perfume faintly lingering on his fingers, bringing her back against his chest, gliding to a soft melody all around the back porch. He remembered their bumping into Luis and Marta, hearing Luis warning Marta not to kiss him, because he had really bad breath. David laughed out loud and spotted his father's eyes in the rear view mirror, spying from behind the steering wheel. His mother asked what he was laughing about. "Nothing," David lied. And mentally returning to Laura's back porch, he wondered how Marta had put up with Luis, especially his body odor.

After the third time Mrs. Oviedo asked her son if a certain schoolmate had attended the party, knowing full well that everyone of them had recently left for the United States, David sat up on the edge of his seat and leaned forward. "Are we leaving?" he asked casually. "Are we going to Miami?" He waited for an answer, shifting his attention between his mother and father.

From that moment until they entered the restaurant, silence prevailed. Crystal chandeliers hung from high ceilings, waiters in tuxedos fastidiously prepared tables with embroidered table linen, silver cutlery, bone china plates, and fresh-cut flowers. A tall, broad-shouldered maitre d' with slicked, jet black hair and a pencil-thin mustache approached David's father. "Good evening and welcome to the Eighteen Hundred Restaurant," he said with a heavy French accent. He introduced himself as Pierre, and, addressing David by name, escorted them into an intimate, dark-wood-paneled private dining room. David asked the Frenchman how he knew his name, and Pierre explained his was the only reservation before nine o'clock. David checked his watch: seven o'clock Pierre then informed David that he was a fortunate young man, because he was dining in the best and most expensive restaurant in Havana.

Once they were alone in the private dining room, David sprang the question again. "Are we leaving?" he asked. "Are we going to Miami?"

His mother and father looked at each other over the tasseled menus printed in French. "David," Mr. Oviedo began. "Your mother and I have decided that it's best to leave the country." He reached over the table and held his wife's hand. "Your mother and I believe that you will have a much better future in the United States than if we stay here. Our country is not what it used to be. When your mother and I were young, there were opportunities in business...a wonderful way of life...but all that is over, and I'm afraid it's only going to get worse."

"It may be hard at first," Mrs. Oviedo added, "but with time, we'll build a good life. You and your brother deserve better than what our country is turning into."

"I..." David began to say, when his father cut him off.

"We understand that at your age this is a difficult change," his father said.

"David," his mother added "we know that leaving your friends will be very hard for you, but you'll make new friends quickly."

From Amigos to Friends

Sitting at the edge of his chair, David was about to speak when a waiter elegantly entered the room. Mr. Oviedo ordered the special of the day for all of them: French onion soup for appetizer, quail a l'orange for the entree and mixed fruit for dessert.

"A wise selection, sir," the waiter respectfully replied out of habit, since it was the only choice available that evening.

"Your mother is right," Mr. Oviedo said as the waiter left the room. "You'll make new friends right away."

"They have wonderful schools in the United States," his mother quickly added.

"With terrific sports programs," his father added.

"You don't even have to wear uniforms to school," she pointed out.

David's attention switched back and forth. "When do we leave?" he asked. "I'm ready. Sounds great!"

David's parents looked at each other. "You're not upset?" they asked simultaneously.

"No, it's exciting," David said. "Will we ever come back to Cuba?"

"Only if Castro falls from power," Mr. Oviedo said.

"That may not happen for many years," Mrs. Oviedo pointed out.

"Do we have to come back when Fidel falls, if we like it a lot in the United States?" David asked.

David's parents again looked at each other quizzically.

"If we really like it in the United States," David said, "it would be better to stay there."

"It makes sense," his father said.

"Where are we going? Miami, New York, Los Angeles?"

The waiter glided into the room carrying a large tray with three cups of steaming French onion soup.

Mr. Oviedo waited for the waiter to leave and then said, "David, your mother and I have to go through some further paperwork before we can get our permits to leave the country." He blew softly on a spoon full of soup and then cautiously brought it to his lips as if buying time. "Your permit arrived this week. You're scheduled to fly to Miami in two weeks. On the thirteenth of October."

"Your father, your brother, and I will join you as soon as possible," she said and braced herself for her son's reaction.

"Why not wait until we can all leave together?" David suggested. "I can wait."

"It's important that you leave for the United States as soon as possible," his father began. "We are concerned that if we wait much longer it may be difficult to get you out of the country."

"Why?" David asked.

"You're going to have to trust us on this," his mother said.

"How about you?" David asked, more concerned by the second.

"We'll get out," his mother assured him. "It may take a little time, but we'll get out."

"The concern is with you," his father explained. "We are worried that the government may stop letting young men out of the country."

"Luis and Carlos will have to stay here?" David asked, choking on his words. "I won't ever see them again?"

"I'm sure you will," his father assured him. "You are very young and the world takes many turns."

"Who am I going to stay with?"

"You'll be staying with a Catholic group that takes care of children who leave Cuba without their parents," his mother said, her voice full of emotion.

"David, your mother and I gave a lot of thought to holding you back until we could all leave together. We're going to miss you terribly, but it's safer this way."

"It won't be for very long," his mother said with tears pooling in her eyes, her hand squeezing her husband's.

David reached out and placed his hand over his parents'. "Mami, don't be upset. It won't be for very long."

Mrs. Oviedo started to cry. She stood up holding a napkin to her face and excused herself to go to the ladies' room.

David and his father sat in silence until his mother returned minutes later.

"I don't want to talk about it anymore tonight," she said. "Let's enjoy our dinner together. We have time after tonight to talk about this."

The waiter entered the room with the entrees.

An hour later, slouched in the back seat of his father's car, looking out the window at the streetlights lining Fifth Avenue, David tried to imagine what it would be like to live in the United States by himself.

What do I do without my parents telling me what to do? Do I get to do anything I want? Right. Dream on. Priests. Nuns. Sunday Mass. To wake up in the morning without my mother stroking my hair. My father won't be there to try to improve my grades. Not to play baseball with Carlos and Luis every day after school. What if they never get out. They're my best friends. Laura. I almost kissed her. I like her a lot. Maybe she'll end up in Miami. I won't be able to see my little brother grow up. To teach him how to play baseball.

He suddenly felt a void in the pit of his stomach. He couldn't think about that. He forced himself to think of Miami. He wished he would start growing soon.

I'm already fourteen and still only five feet, two inches and one-hundred-five pounds. In the United States everybody's tall and strong, like John Wayne. Girls don't like short, skinny boys. I'll lift weights. I'll eat like a horse. I'll drink all the milk and take all the vitamins I can get my hands on. And I want to get a big motorcycle. Blue. Red's too flashy. With a good back seat to ride girls around. Tall, blond American women like the ones in the movies, but my age.

He felt selfish and decided he would work after school to save enough money to buy his parents a car when they arrived. He'd buy them a '57 Chevy—blue, of course. A two-tone: dark blue top with a baby blue bottom.

The car stopped, and he felt his father's hand softly shaking his shoulder. "Wake up, David," his father said. "We're home."

Inside, David threw his clothes on the floor and slipped under the sheets.

What am I going to tell Carlos and Luis in the morning? What do I say about maybe never seeing them again?

Five minutes later, he was asleep. He tossed and turned all night.

At the crack of dawn the next day, David sneaked out of his garage and quietly pushed his motorcycle out onto the street. He parked in Carlos' driveway, knowing that his friend would recognize the sound of his engine. Carlos came out onto the balcony in his pajamas with Rocky by his side.

"CODE RED!" David called out.

Carlos rushed back inside the house. David went to Luis' house. He jumped the side fence and peeped in Luis' sister's window, hoping she would be lying naked in bed; instead, he found her head covered with curlers and a sheet up to her nose. He went to Luis' window and called out "CODE RED!" Luis jumped out of bed in his boxer shorts and bolted for his closet. David retraced his steps and mounted his motorcycle.

Five minutes later, David waited for his best friends at the motorcycle club, rehearsing his opening line. He knew they would not be far behind. "Code Red" stood for "maximum level emergency" and required convening at the club within eleven minutes—maximum. The code had never been used before.

From Amigos to Friends

Luis arrived first, his black T-shirt inside out, his fly open and the laces of his black high-top sneakers undone. He ran into the room and flopped on the couch. Before he had recovered his breath to ask what had triggered the "Code Red," Carlos flew in, his hair sticking straight up, no shoes, shirt badly buttoned and drool hanging down his chin.

"This better be Code Red material!" he warned David and crashed on the floor.

"It better be!" Luis agreed.

"I can't believe it! You think I would take the Code Red lightly," David said, springing up from the couch. "I invented Code Red!"

"Get it out!" Carlos said.

"This better be important!" Luis said.

David took a deep breath and, standing in front of his friends, said, "I'm leaving. I'm going to Miami."

The room stayed perfectly still for what seemed an eternity.

Carlos suddenly jumped up, rushed to David, wrapped his arms around him, and knocked him down. "Lucky! You lucky dog!" he kept yelling while he locked his friend in a bear hug. David struggled to get loose.

"Stop it!" Luis said, loudly.

David broke loose and got halfway down the room before Carlos dove for his ankle and brought him down.

"Stop it!" Luis screamed. "Stop it!"

David and Carlos stopped wrestling and from the floor looked back toward Luis, who was sitting on the floor against the couch. He had his chin on his knees and his arms tightly wrapped around his legs.

"What's the matter with you?" Carlos asked.

"What's wrong, Luis?" David asked.

"Nothing," Luis said.

"Are you mad or something?" David asked.

"What's wrong now, Luis?" Carlos asked.

"Nothing," he repeated.

David sat down next to Luis. "What's the matter?" David asked. "Why are you so upset?"

"I don't understand why both of you are so happy about you leaving," said Luis finally, reluctantly.

"It's exciting. It's an adventure," Carlos said. "New things, new people. The United States has everything. It's the home of rock-and-roll."

"You're not going to the United States, Carlos," Luis said, "so why are you so excited about it?"

Carlos stood up and started circling the room. "I'm getting out of this island," he began. "There's nothing here that I want..."

"How about your parents?" Luis interrupted.

"Of course I want my mother," Carlos kicked Luis' leg. "I'll convince my mother to go to the United States. She'll drag the rest of the family along."

"Are you afraid that Carlos and I will leave," David said, "and you'll end up here in Cuba by yourself? Is that why you're upset?"

Luis looked away.

Carlos sat back down on the other side of Luis and said, "That's it, isn't it, Luis? That's why you're upset. You're jealous!"

"Eat shit, Carlos!" Luis blurted out.

"Carlos, you're such an ass," David said.

"You guys would feel the same way," Luis said. "I want to go too, but can you see my father letting me go to the United States? No way."

"He can't force you to stay!" Carlos said.

"Carlos, don't be stupid," Luis said. "Of course he can. He's my father."

"He doesn't live with you," Carlos said in self-defense.

"He's still my father!"

"He can't keep you a prisoner your whole life," Carlos pointed out. "When you become an adult you can go anywhere you want."

"I'm fourteen, Carlos," Luis said. "What am I going to do for the next four years?"

"Is that when you become an adult?" David asked. "I think you're wrong, Luis. I think you become an adult at twenty-one, not eighteen. That would make it seven years."

"Thanks a lot, David," Luis said.

"Shut up, David," Carlos said. "You're making it worse."

"I only wanted to clarify the facts," David said.

"You always want to be right," Carlos said to David.

"I do not," David said. "I'm only trying to help."

"Well, try something different," Carlos said, "because all you're doing is making things worse."

They were quiet for a long time, staring at nothing in particular, until David sprang to his feet, startling his friends. "I got it!" he said.

"Now what?" Carlos asked, looking up.

David began circling the motorcycle club. One wall was covered with spare engine parts: pistons, piston rings, crankshafts. The rest of the walls were decorated with motorcycle racing posters, featuring motorcycles and drivers in heart-stopping actions.

As his plan finally jelled, David faced Luis. "Your mother can sneak you out of the country, Luis," David said with authority.

Carlos and Luis looked at each other. Carlos started laughing first. Luis started laughing even louder. They fed on each other's laughter until they were on their backs howling.

"Hey, Luis," Carlos said, trying to control his laughter. "I can just see your mother rowing to Miami to drop you off. And being back by morning for breakfast."

Carlos and Luis exploded with laughter. David stood his ground.

"Better yet," Luis said, holding onto his side, trying hard not to laugh, "she can take me to the beach one night, put me in the water and I can dog paddle to Miami."

Carlos and Luis again roared with laughter. "Stop laughing, Luis," Carlos said, laughing and holding onto his side. "I can't take it any longer."

"If you two morons would listen to me," David said, "you might find it entirely possible."

Carlos and Luis had another attack of laughter.

"Please, David," Carlos said, "don't make me laugh anymore. I can't take it any longer." He wiped drool from his mouth.

"I'm serious," David said. "Listen to me!"

Luis stopped laughing long enough to say, "Go ahead, David. I can't wait to hear this."

"Not until you guys stop acting spastic," David said.

Carlos and Luis burst out laughing again. "Look who's talking about acting spastic!" Carlos said.

David went to the door. "I'm leaving," he said. "The hell with you guys!"

Carlos went after David. "Wait! Wait!" he said. "I want to hear it."

"Let him go, Carlos," Luis said. "Can't you see he's crazy."

"Shut up, Luis," Carlos said. "Don't be a baby, David. Sit down."

David left the door and sat with Carlos and Luis.

"I'm leaving by myself," David said. Carlos and Luis became very serious. "Maybe your mother can make all the preparations without your father finding out, and then she can send you to the United States by yourself."

"I wouldn't go along with that," Luis said. "He would kill my mother."

"Are you really leaving for the United States by yourself?" Carlos asked.

"Yes," David said. "My parents don't have their exit visas yet. Something about paperwork."

Carlos paced the room. "This is interesting," he said. "I can go to the United States without my family."

"Carlos, that's terrible!" Luis said.

"Yeah, Carlos," David said. "Your own parents."

"You're leaving without your family," Carlos pointed out to David.

"But not by choice," David said in self-defense.

"I'm almost fifteen years old," Carlos said. "I'm ready to be on my own."

"You're full of shit, Carlos," Luis said.

"I can't help it if you're immature, Luis," Carlos said.

Luis went to the door. "Carlos, you're a selfish jerk. I wouldn't leave my family behind for anything."

"I don't have any choice, Luis," David said, defensively. "My parents want me to go. They say it's for the best."

"I'm sure it is, David," Luis said sarcastically and left.

David went after him.

"Let him go, David!"

David stopped at the door. He turned around and stared out into emptiness.

"Don't let him spoil it for you," Carlos said. "He's upset because he can't go."

"Do you really think so?" David asked.

"He would crawl to the airport to catch a flight to Miami if he had the chance," Carlos said.

"I want to go. I'm excited to go, but I'm scared." David sat down on the couch. Carlos sat down on the floor in front of him.

"What are you scared about?" Carlos asked.

David hesitated.

"Come on, David. We've been friends since kindergarten."

"What if I never see my parents again? My brother... Luis... you? What if I'm the only one to leave?" David looked away, trying to hide a tear.

Carlos looked away.

The room remained still.

Carlos then sprang to his feet. "No way. I don't know about the others, but I'll leave. Even if I have to swim all the way to Miami."

Carlos jumped on top of David and started tickling him. They wrestled until Carlos surrendered, just before David pulled Carlos' arm so far behind his back it almost broke.

Luis tucked his shirttail in, zipped up his fly, and tied his shoelaces before he went into his house. In the kitchen, he found his mother washing the breakfast dishes.

"Sit down, Luisito. Here's a glass of chocolate milk and some toast," his mother said.

"David is leaving for Miami," he said. "Mami, I don't want to stay behind, alone."

"I understand," she said. "I understand."

"I'm sure Carlos will leave soon."

Luis reluctantly dipped a slice of buttered toast in a tall glass of cold chocolate milk and slowly chewed on the bread.

"Mami, is there any chance that Papi would let me go to the United States? Would he?" Luis saw tears in his mother's eyes. "Forget I said that, Mami. I wouldn't want to go without you. I'm sorry I said it."

"Luisito, don't feel bad," she said with the apron by her eyes. "I understand how you feel. Yes, I would send you and your sister to the United States by yourselves, because it's best for you. But your father would never allow it."

"Mami, if there was a way," he said, "would you leave with us and leave Papi behind?"

"No, I wouldn't," she said firmly and quickly, as if she had answered the question before.

"But Papi doesn't even live with us."

"Not now, but he will one day. Soon, I hope."

Luis remained silent while his mother cried behind her apron. His stomach was tight and had a burning sensation. He felt like crying, but he refused to.

"Luisito," his mother said, composing herself, "you have to keep what I'm about to say between us. Can I count on that?" She paused and Luis nodded. "You have to understand that before the Revolution your father was never able to make any headway. The Revolution has made it possible for him to be somebody. He'll never leave Cuba, and I won't go without him."

"I understand, Mami," Luis said.

"When you grow up, I would not blame you if you left. I would miss you a lot, but I would understand," she said in tears. Luis jumped out of his seat and flung his arms around her.

———

Carlos went to the back yard and sat down in the grass. Susie nestled on his lap, and Rocky heeled by his side. Carlos threw himself around Rocky's neck, careful not to squash Susie. "I'm going to miss the both of you," he said. Rocky started howling as if he understood.

Carlos found his mother in the foyer, giving the final touches to a flower arrangement on an entry table. "Carlitos, I've been worried to death. Where have you been? You didn't even have breakfast." She started for the kitchen. "I'll have the maid make you a snack."

Carlos blocked her way. "Mami, David is leaving for Miami. I want to leave right away."

Mrs. Fernández braced herself on the wall with one hand and covered her mouth with her other hand.

"Why haven't we left yet?" he demanded to know. "What are we waiting for?"

"Your father and I don't want to leave," she said, trying to control herself.

"I'll go by myself then!" He stood in front of his mother with his arms crossed and a pout on his face.

"Carlitos, how can you say that?" Her eyes filled up with tears. "You're breaking my heart."

"All you care about is what you want. You don't care about me."

"You're my life. You're the most important thing to me," she said with tears streaming down her cheeks. "How can you say those terrible things?"

"I don't care. I want to go."

Mrs. Fernández slapped her son, erasing the pout from his face. Carlos went around her and ran out the front door. The door slammed hard against its frame.

Mrs. Fernández marched upstairs. She entered her bedroom crying and slammed the door behind her.

"What's wrong with you?" her husband asked. He was lying down in bed reading the newspaper in his white boxer shorts, undershirt, and black socks. "What's with all the slamming doors?"

She threw herself on the bed next to him. "I just did a terrible thing," she said, crying into her pillow. "It's all your fault."

"What did you do?" he asked, without taking his eyes off the sports section.

"I slapped Carlitos. My dear Carlitos!"

"Good!" he said from behind the paper. "It's about time. I'm sure he earned it."

"He wants to go to Miami right away," she said, sobbing, "without me if I won't go along."

"Terrific idea," he said, putting the paper down. "Going by himself will make a man out of him."

She stopped crying. Her tears were now replaced by hostility. "How could you even think that? You're a monster!"

"He's almost fifteen years old," he pointed out, attacking back. "He's only a little boy in your eyes."

She quickly got out of bed. "You don't love him," she said, accusingly. "You're jealous of him. You want to get rid of him."

Mr. Fernández angrily returned to the sports section. "I'm not discussing this any further," he said from behind the paper. "You're hysterical."

"I'm not hysterical!" she screamed, ripping the newspaper out of his hands. "I want us to move to Miami. Right away!"

He sprang out of bed and ripped the shredded newspaper out of her hand. "I'm not going to let that spoiled brat control my life. We're staying right where we are."

"You're a selfish man!" she said, accusingly. "It's not just your son. It's your daughter's life you're gambling..."

"Don't be melodramatic!"

"Melodramatic? You were here. You saw the soldiers. The machine guns. She was spared by a miracle from God." She looked up and respectfully made the sign of the cross.

"Not to mention my charm and sense of humor."

"Please, forgive him, Lord." Again she made the sign of the cross.

"Why don't you pray for Fidel to die instead? That would solve all our problems."

"You don't love any of us. You want to stay here to torture us."

"I've told you before," he said, controlling his temper, "I'm not going to start all over again. To leave everything behind. I've worked like a dog all my life, and I'm not going to leave it all behind."

"They're leaving," she said. "Why..."

"He's an architect. She's a doctor!" he interrupted her, his body tense, his hands making tight fists. "I don't have what it takes to start with nothing in the United States. I don't even speak a word of English."

She took two slow steps and embraced him. He held her tight against him and said, "You can go with the kids. I wouldn't blame you. Maybe it's best for all of us."

She didn't answer.

CHAPTER XI

The boys had agreed to meet the next day at the motorcycle club. David arrived early, anxious to absorb and retain as much of his present life as possible. He parked in the garage behind a heavy iron gate. Slowly, he went up the spiral staircase one step at a time, instead of running up two steps at a time as he usually did. Reaching the top landing, he stopped and scanned the rooftops and mature trees all around him. Above him, the early morning sun flexed its young muscles, vaporizing delicate beads of morning dew on tree leaves. He took a deep breath and inhaled the aroma from the strong Cuban coffee brewing in Carlos' grandmother's kitchen. In the distance, a series of roosters competed for the honor of delivering the loudest and most elaborate announcement of the new day. A soft draft caressed his forehead, like his mother did every morning while sitting on the edge of his bed. "The first day of the rest of your life," David heard his mother whispering in his mind. "Make it count."

Inside the club, his eyes slowly took inventory. He realized the couch was dark orange and not brown, and that it had a small tear on top of the left armrest. A cockroach darted across the room without stirring his instinct to squash it under his foot. He took from the wall a brand new, shiny spare piston for his engine. He had searched long and hard to procure it, never realizing he would not need it.

"You're here early," Carlos said, walking in and disturbing David's reverie. "Boy, do I have news for you."

David hung the piston back on the wall. "What?" David asked.

"You're not the only one going to Miami," Carlos said without any emotion.

"All right!" David cheered. "When do you leave?" He went over and slapped Carlos' back.

"I don't know yet," Carlos said. "My mother says it may take a while to get our exit permits."

"Are your parents going to send you out first, like my parents are doing?"

"No, the plan is for my mother, my sister, and me to leave together as soon as possible."

"How about your father?"

Carlos looked away. "He'll join us later. That's what my mother said this morning," Carlos paused, "but I don't believe her. I think he wants us to leave so he can get rid of us."

"Carlos! Do you really believe that? Why would your father want to do that?"

"Because he's in love with another woman."

They looked at each other in silence, until they heard Luis running up the spiral staircase.

Luis walked in, studied their faces, looked around the room and said, "Where's the dead body?"

"What do you mean?" David asked.

"You guys look so serious, I thought maybe you were holding a funeral."

Luis was the only one to laugh at his own joke.

"It's not funny, Luis," David said.

"What's so damn serious?" Luis asked.

"Nobody laughs when you're having problems, Luis," David said. "You're not the only one with tragedies in your life."

"That's right," Carlos said, trapping Luis between David and himself. "You're not the only one."

"When you're hurting, everyone is supposed to drop every-thing and feel sorry for you and help you out," David continued. "Poor little Luis this, poor little Luis that!"

"That's right," Carlos agreed. "That's all we're supposed to do, feel bad for you. It's my turn now. I deserve some atten-tion, too!"

Luis threw his arms up in the air. "Okay, okay," he said. "I surrender. I'm guilty, even though I don't know why."

"I'm leaving for Miami," Carlos started to tell Luis, "with-out..."

Luis interrupted. "Why is that bad? Yesterday..."

David jumped in. "Luis, why don't you shut up and listen for a change?"

"My father is not going. He's staying..." Carlos' voice cracked and did not complete the sentence. He went to the couch and collapsed.

Luis looked at David and, with a shrug, asked him for the rest of the story. David's eyes checked with Carlos and he got the go-ahead.

"Carlos thinks his father is in love with another woman and is staying behind to be with her and get rid of them."

"Do you really believe that?" Luis asked, sitting next to Carlos.

"I know it for a fact," Carlos said.

"No way," David said. He dropped on the floor in front of the couch. "How do you know?"

"I've heard him on the phone talking to her."

"No!" David said.

"What did he say?" Luis asked.

"He said that my mother is fat and ugly..."

David interrupted. "She may be a little bit overweight, but she's not fat."

"Your mother is beautiful. She has beautiful green eyes," Luis said.

"I know. They're just like mine," Carlos continued. "I heard him say that one day they would be together. That being with us was only a duty for the time being."

"Who is she?" David asked.

"Her name is Linda. She works for my father."

"What does she look like?" Luis asked.

"She's a tall mulatto with big tits and a fat ass." Carlos went to the window. "I don't care if he stays here. I'm going to Miami. The sooner, the better."

"Can you guys keep a secret?" Luis said. The question peeled Carlos away from the window.

"Of course," David lied.

"For life," Carlos lied.

"There's a pretty good chance that I'll be joining you guys in the United States," Luis lied. "That's it. I can't say anymore."

Carlos and David leaped on top of Luis. They pinned him on the floor and wouldn't stop twisting his arm until Luis told them a big lie about his father being secretly against the Revolution and getting ready to leave for the United States, just like their parents.

After repeating the big lie three times, Luis made them promise to write to each other at least once a month until they were together again. The commitment was sealed when each one accepted their mother's death out loud as fair punishment for breaking their pact. Struggling with the burning desire to tell them what his parents had said about perhaps being too late for Carlos and Luis to leave Cuba, David kept it to himself. He did not want to hurt his best friends, and, most of all, he did not want to accept the possibility that he might never see them again.

The rest of the morning was spent debating a multitude of subjects, starting with where would be best to live in the United States. Carlos picked New York or Tennessee. New

York because of the night life and Tennessee because that's where Elvis lived. Luis chose New York because that's where they published most mystery books, or Hollywood where they made horror films. David settled on California because of the weather. All three agreed that Miami was their last choice because it would be full of Cubans. Why leave the island and end up in the same place again?

Selecting a woman was a much more serious subject and took a lot longer to debate, especially with Carlos changing his mind every five minutes and explaining in detail why his new choice was better. He finally settled on Jayne Mansfield, "for no particular reason," he said, denying it had anything to do with the fact that she had a bigger chest than all the runners-up. Luis, partial to darker women, and because he had heard Latin women were sexually deviant, excluding his mother, of course, chose Sophia Loren. David's choice of Brigitte Bardot drew cool reviews from the critics. They agreed that she was pretty and had a sexy voice. Being French was definitely a plus, and being funny added to her score, but David stood alone in giving her high marks for her figure. The critics could not articulate why, but Brigitte Bardot was not quite in the same league with Jayne Mansfield and Sophia Loren.

The morning ended with Luis coming up with the idea of carving their names on the wall paneling and then impressing Carlos and David by pulling a six-inch switchblade out of his pocket.

The evening before David was to leave Cuba, his mother made every effort to make their last meal together as normal as possible. Mrs. Oviedo had María prepare all of David's favorites. Sitting at the dining room table watching her son devour his favorite dinner, she picked at her own food. Her eyes were red and swollen from crying all afternoon while sewing name tags to his clothes and packing the one small suitcase her son was allowed to take out of the country. María had taken his brother to the park all afternoon to isolate him from his mother's grief. All day long she had relived many moments she had shared with her oldest and for so many years her only son. She now regretted the decision she and her husband had reached to let David leave on a journey that could separate them for life. She had finally stopped crying two hours earlier when she heard David storm into the house. She had promised herself that she would not make a spectacle and leave her son with the memory of a sad, helpless woman. She wanted her son to leave without fears, without guilt, without an emotional ball-and-chain from having left a crying mother behind.

"Mami, I don't want David to go," his brother said with a mouth full of fruit cocktail.

Mrs. Oviedo buried her face behind a napkin, excused herself, and quickly left the room. Mr. Oviedo left the table after his wife. María rushed from the kitchen and took his brother down from the highchair to finish dinner in the kitchen. His father returned after a few minutes and told David that his mother wasn't feeling well and, since they had to get up so early to go to the airport the next morning, she was going to turn in for the evening.

"Papi, is it possible that you won't be able to get out, and I may not see you and Mami again?" David asked, losing his appetite.

"It's not probable, but possible."

"If that happens, I'll come back."

"That would hurt your mother and me more than never seeing you again. Son, promise me you'll never come back unless Fidel falls and Cuba is a free country again."

"But..."

"If you came back, all the suffering would have been in vain. Promise me you won't."

"I promise," David said, reluctantly. "I promise."

"Your mother, brother, and I should be joining you in about six months."

"Why so long?"

"Your mother and I are both professionals with the type of training that the government doesn't want to part with. Especially with your mother being a doctor of internal medicine. A lot of medical doctors have left the country already. I'm not telling you this to alarm you. I'm telling you the facts. You're almost a man now and I'm treating you like one."

"How do you know you're going to be able to get out then?"

Mr. Oviedo looked toward the kitchen door, hesitated and signaled for David to follow him. They went out through the living room's ten-foot high, sliding glass doors, onto the interior patio. They sat across from each other, their facial features softly lit by the landscape lighting. Through the big leaves of the breadfruit tree that shaded most of the interior patio, the sky was pinpointed with sparkling stars. The night air was warm and carried the smell of impending rain. The songs of frogs and crickets broke the quietness of the night.

"About four months ago," Mr. Oviedo began, "a perfect stranger walked into the store. David, you must keep this a complete secret. Our joining you in the United States is at stake."

"I promise," David quickly said. He leaned forward from the edge of his chair, his eyes wide open.

"After he spent a long time browsing through all the books, he bought a book on seventeenth-century Flemish art. I joked with him that I had expected that it would be the last book to go before I retired or ran out of books to sell. He laughed, and we spent the rest of the morning—you know how slow it is during the weekdays—talking about art and books. During the next three weeks, he dropped by the store a couple of mornings a week to talk. Once he learned about my background from questions he asked and from checking me out,

I'm sure, he told me that his real function at the Ministry of Culture was to export Communist propaganda..."

"What does that have to do with your getting out of Cuba?" David asked.

"He's in charge of a department that brings magazines into Cuba from Russia with what he calls "soft propaganda." For example, a Russian magazine that's the equivalent of *Life* magazine, except it's published to softly sell the Russian version of the world. He has proposed facilitating our exit to the United States in exchange for my help in Miami to get these magazines into the United States."

"Would you do that?" David said, sitting back.

"No, it would be dishonest and against everything that I stand for. However," his father said, "I'm going to play along with it to get us out of the country. Then, when we're in the United States, I'll walk away from it."

"Isn't that dangerous?" David asked.

"Not any more dangerous than staying here, or crossing ninety miles of open sea in a small boat." His father paused. "You remember that they arrested me for no particular reason during the invasion."

"Don't you worry that they would try to get even when you get to Miami and you don't follow through?"

"David, this is small stuff. This is not like the movies. It's not top-secret issues, but soft propaganda magazines. I'm sure they already have many other ways of getting them into the U.S."

"Does Mami know about this?"

"Every detail."

David sat back with a worried look on his face.

"I'm telling you all this not to worry you, but to show you that we are doing everything possible to get out of Cuba to be with you as soon as possible. You also know how careful and deliberate your mother and I are, so be assured we're not going to do anything irrational."

"I know. I trust your judgment."

"Thank you, son. I trust that you'll use good judgment in everything that you do while you're not under your mother's and my supervision."

"I will."

"It's easy to say, son. But it's going to challenge your character. Being by yourself at this young age is going to be a very demanding challenge. You're going to be in many new situations. Since you're going to have to make many decisions without our input and counsel, I want you to promise me you'll always ask yourself how your mother and I would feel about your actions."

"I will. I promise."

"At your age, one wrong step and you could jeopardize your whole future."

"I'll be careful. I promise."

"Remember what your mother always tells you. Your actions are a reflection of your family." Mr. Oviedo stood up and opened his arms. David buried himself in his father's hug. "I love you, David. I love you, son. Please be careful until we get there."

"I love you, Papi. I'll be careful. I promise."

David tossed and turned all night as his body reacted to many dreams and outright nightmares. In the middle of the night he opened his eyes and heard his mother's voice. "Wake up, David, you're having a nightmare."

He felt her hand on his forehead, then softly stroking his hair. David realized his body was covered with sweat. She sat at the edge of his bed in her pink silk nightgown. It was dark, except for a light in the hallway connecting their rooms. "Were you having a bad dream?" she asked.

David nodded.

"Do you want to talk about it?"

David shook his head. "I'm sorry I woke you up, Mami."

"You didn't," she said and kissed his forehead. "I've been having bad dreams myself."

"Do you want to talk about it?" David smiled.

She softly pulled on his hair and shook her head, smiling.

"I'm glad we woke up," she said, "because I've been wanting to tell you how much I'm going to miss you, but I've been afraid that I would start crying so hard that I would get you all upset." Her voice cracked and her eyes pooled with tears.

David held her hand. "I'm not going to get upset if you cry," he said. "It's okay for girls to cry." He smiled, knowing how she would respond.

"There's nothing wrong with boys crying either. It's healthy to cry. I've always told you to cry if you feel like crying. It won't make you any less of a man." Her tears now dripped from her cheeks.

David nodded with tears in his eyes. "I'm going to miss you, Mami. I love you very much."

His mother leaned down and hugged him. "I love you so much. I'm going to miss you every second we're apart. I promise you that no matter what, we won't be apart for long."

She leaned back. The hallway light allowed their eyes to make contact. "Promise me you're going to be good and stay out of trouble," she said.

"I will. I'll make you proud."

⚊⚊⚊

As the first soft rays of light pierced through the darkness, David quietly tiptoed into his baby brother's room, and for a few seconds observed him asleep on his stomach, wearing only a white cloth diaper. David softly kissed his fat face, and quietly joined his parents in the garage. At the door, he traded kisses with a crying María. Minutes later, they picked up Carlos and Luis.

From Amigos to Friends

In the back seat, the three young men traded jokes, old stories, dreams, aspirations, and promises, all at high speed, propelled by the awareness that time was passing and very soon life would cease to exist as it had for as far back as they could remember.

In the front seat, Mr. Oviedo drove in silence with his left hand on the steering wheel and his right hand tightly around both of his wife's hands, resting on her lap.

They arrived at José Martí International Airport twenty minutes later as the sun broke over the horizon. Once inside the small terminal, their personal experience blended with those of the families and friends of the one hundred Cubans who were gathered to board that day's Pan American Airlines twin-prop DC-3 flight. After less than forty-five minutes in the air, they would be transported from their homeland, family, and friends to Miami. There, they would begin new lives with all the benefits of living in the wealthiest, most democratic country in the world. Their challenge would be to carve out for themselves a decent present and a prosperous future, despite the hardship of a new language and culture. Most would arrive in the United States with only the clothes they wore, a small suitcase, and a rudimentary knowledge of the English language.

Soldiers in fatigue uniforms and armed with automatic weapons kept a suspicious, contemptuous eye on the suffering civilians. Shoulder to shoulder, family and friends wept over the impending separations. Grandparents held small children dressed in miniature suits and Sunday dresses, who didn't understand why their grandparents wept and said farewell to their parents and to them. Mr. Oviedo kept his group from being separated by the constant pushing and shoving. Mrs. Oviedo stood behind David with her arms around his shoulders. Carlos and Luis were pressed against him by the crowd.

Over the loudspeaker, a crackling voice ordered all passengers to immediately enter the next room via a set of double glass doors. Any passenger not in the room within five minutes would not be allowed to leave the country. A wall of thick glass separated the two rooms. The crowd moved with a jolt. Fear spread throughout. They were swept toward the double doors. They clung to each other. "Don't push! Don't push! Please don't push!" they heard throughout the crowd. But they kept moving as if caught up in an invisible current. Mr. Oviedo firmly handed David his passport with the airline ticket and exit permit tucked inside. "Hold onto it tightly. Don't let it out of your hands until you get to Miami!"

David took the passport in one hand and with the other hung on to his mother. They were getting pushed closer to the door. David saw two huge soldiers, one black and one white, shoving passengers holding airline tickets past the door and shoving everyone else aside.

Mr. Oviedo threw his arms around his son and kissed him on the cheek. "I love you, son. Take good care of yourself. Write us a letter as soon as you can."

David felt Carlos and Luis pat him on the shoulder and heard their reminders to write. Ten feet from the soldiers, David clung to his mother and she clung to her son. They kept moving, propelled by the crowd rushing to meet the five-minute deadline. Mrs. Oviedo's eyes were a river of tears.

"David," his father said, "go inside and stand against the glass." With one motion, Mr. Oviedo separated mother and son at the last second before the soldier shoved David through the door. David immediately began squeezing his way toward the glass wall. On the other side, Mr. Oviedo led the way, with Carlos' and Luis' help, to secure a place by the glass.

After much pushing and shoving on both sides, they finally stood in front of each other, separated from head to toe by an inch of glass.

For over an hour, his father, mother, Carlos, and Luis traded places to communicate with David by sign language, until they heard the announcement to board. David stuck his passport under his belt and planted both palms against the glass, one against his father's hand and one on his mother's.

Outside, as he reluctantly moved down the tarmac toward the plane and later from his window seat, he waved at the crowd that frantically waved back from the airport's rooftop observation deck. But, as hard as he tried, until the airplane took off, David's teary eyes never found his family or friends in the crowd.

CHAPTER XII

A shiver raked David's back the moment the plane touched down. "Welcome to Miami," announced a stewardess, igniting an emotional outburst of clapping, whistling, crying, praying, laughing.

"Thank you, my God!"

"Down with Fidel!"

"We're finally free!"

Getting off the plane took forever because so many passengers threw themselves on the tarmac to kiss the ground of their new homeland. It was cold and raining, as if David had traveled north fifteen hundred miles instead of the two hundred miles separating Havana and Miami.

David entered the immigration building, and the first person he encountered was a priest. "Are you arriving alone?" the priest, Father Michael, asked him. The word "alone" cracked David's composure, and only the presence next to the priest of a frightened ten-year-old girl protecting her six-year-old brother, who held on tightly to his sister's waist, kept David from breaking down on the spot.

They left the immigration building after having his passport stamped: "INDEFINITE VOLUNTARY DEPARTURE—STUDENT." David trailed Father Michael through the airport parking lot loaded down with the brother's and sister's luggage plus his own bag. The Irish priest with a weathered face carried the sobbing little boy in his arms, while he kept assuring the boy's sister, walking by his side with a firm grip on his cossack, that her brother was not going to die as she kept predicting. Exhausted, they reached the priest's 1960 Chevy Impala station wagon and headed out of the airport under the cover of ominous dark clouds. The sobbing and wailing from the brother and sister in the back seat, together with concern for Father Michael, who appeared on the verge of a heart attack, discouraged David from the temptation to turn on the radio and catch a few tunes on WFUN, as he had so often done on Carlos' shortwave radio.

They stopped for lunch at a Burger King. The experience was ruined for David when the priest announced that because it was Friday, the only item David could order from the otherwise mouth-watering, wall-mounted menu was a fish burger. A fish burger? The crying brats got to order whatever they wanted—Father Michael's way of shutting them up. David resented it, but after ten minutes of quiet, he began to appreciate the wisdom of the priest's decision.

Shortly after lunch, they dropped off the girl at a Sisters of Mercy school for girls, where it took two beefy nuns and Father Michael to split the siblings apart. As they drove away, David moved to the back seat to comfort the little boy who was crying his eyes out. David held the little kid as if he were his baby brother, until they left the boy with an elderly couple from Santiago de Cuba, the boy's hometown.

The wrinkled priest then carried on a twenty-minute monologue, questioning what sin had he committed to deserve, after forty-two years of faithful service to God and Church, the daily burden of carting broken-hearted children from the airport to foster homes. "I'm too old for this," he lamented.

The station wagon pulled in front of two dinky, nondescript houses on a treeless neighborhood street. Several Cuban teenaged boys hung around the front yard. David noticed that all of them were older and dressed much more "American" than he was. The vehicle pulled into the driveway and the teenagers approached the station wagon. After disinterested glances at David, they returned to their boredom.

Inside one of the houses, Father Michael introduced David to Mr. Martínez, a middle-aged man whose belly made him appear pregnant, and to Mrs. Martínez, who would have been attractive if not for her mustache. Father Michael explained to David that the Martínezes worked for the Catholic Church, supervising the sixteen teenaged Cuban boys living with them in the house. Sixteen more lived next door under the supervision of another Cuban couple.

Father Michael then blessed David and the Martínezes in hyper-speed Latin and bolted out the front door.

Mr. Martínez led David down a narrow, dark hallway. Three bunk beds were crammed into a bedroom half the size of David's room in Havana. David wondered how to reach the lower bunk Mr. Martínez assigned to him. Squeezing between the wall and one of the beds, David reached the closet that Mr. Martínez said was one-sixth his. Adding anything inside the closet seemed unlikely to David, but he pushed, shoved, and finally wedged his suitcase inside the closet. In front of a tiny bathroom, Mr. Martínez informed David that because the house had only three bathrooms, and one was for the exclusive use of the Martínezes, the sixteen teenagers shared two bathrooms.

"This bathroom is for your use between six-ten and six-twenty in the morning," said Mr. Martínez, reading from a schedule posted next to the bathroom door while he crossed out a name and scribbled David's in its place. "... And from eight-fifteen to eight-thirty at night." Mr. Martínez then looked down sternly at David. "When there's no one scheduled, it's first come, first served. I suggest you stay within your allotted time. They'll lynch you if you hold things up."

Mrs. Martínez then joined them. "Take good care of this," she said, issuing David a threadbare piece of cloth. David tried very hard not to stare at her mustache. "You only get one towel a week."

The rest of the afternoon consisted of learning more rules and being subjected to the scrutiny of a long, slow parade of guys trickling in from school and stopping by to check David out. They all asked the same two questions: "Where in Cuba are you from?" and "How old are you?" If the question was from someone also from Havana, two more questions followed: "What school did you go to?" and "What private club did you belong to?" David didn't know any of the thirty-one guys and he ended up being the youngest and smallest of the entire group.

At six o'clock in the afternoon, the living room was converted into a large dining room as the boys brought in wood benches and chairs from the back yard. Dinner was then served a whole two hours earlier than at David's house in Havana. "The American way," he was informed by a guy who acted like a veteran because he had arrived a week earlier. All thirty-two teenagers ate dinner together under the stern discipline of Mr. Martínez and Mr. López.

That first night in the United States, lying wide awake in his bunk with all the lights out, David heard scattered sobbing throughout the dormitory. Pressing the pillow against his ears, he held back tears. Thinking about his parents and his brother, he wanted to cry, but did not allow himself.

From now until my parents arrive, I have to act like a man. That's what my parents expect of me. That's what I'll do. It's what Papi would do.

<hr>

After being dropped off by David's parents, the boys decided to spend the day at the beach. Although Mr. Oviedo had invited them to stay for lunch upon their arrival back in Miramar, the boys had politely declined, enumerating a string of lame, unrelated excuses that Mr. Oviedo accepted graciously. Not a word had been uttered during the entire drive back from the airport. David's mother had cried while her husband drove as if in a trance. In the back seat, Carlos and Luis silently stared out their individual windows.

A huge fight erupted between Carlos and Luis when Luis insisted that they go to the "Bottle" beach after Carlos had suggested spending the day at the club. Luis accused Carlos of only wanting to go to the club to be with Silvia. Carlos, of course, denied it and then relented, proving to Luis that he was still "a free spirit." They drove their motorcycles to the public beach. Luis arrived ten minutes ahead of Carlos by running every red light and every stopsign.

"What are you trying to do?" Carlos said when he finally caught up with Luis. "... kill yourself before we get to join David in Miami."

Skipping lunch, having lost their appetite after seeing their best friend fly out of their lives, allowed them to go in the ocean right away. Luis ran at full speed into the water and he furiously swam to the Bottle as if his life depended on it. From the sand, Carlos saw Luis climb at neck-breaking speed the twenty feet up to the very top of the bottle. When he reached the top, Luis skipped the usual several seconds composure time and instead flung himself, headfirst, off the Bottle. Carlos held his breath and used body English to guide Luis through the air past the concrete deck all the way into the safety of the water below. Carlos flopped down on the sand, realizing that Luis' head had barely missed the concrete deck.

When Luis swam back to shore, Carlos looked the other way.

"Aren't you coming in the water?" Luis asked.

Carlos refused to acknowledge his presence.

"What's the matter with you?" Luis asked.

Carlos left the water's edge and took a stool at a rustic, thatched-roofed bar on the sand twenty feet from the water.

He ordered a lemonade. Luis joined him and shocked Carlos by ordering an Hatuey beer and having the bartender serve it to him. Luis again tried to start a casual conversation. And again Carlos refused to participate.

After they drank their drinks in silence, Luis said, "I miss him already."

"Is that why you're acting so crazy?"

"Just blowing off some steam," Luis said, shrugging it off.

"It looks more like you're trying to blow yourself off this planet."

"I'm just being myself."

"Who are you trying to impress drinking a beer?"

"I can't help it if I'm more mature than you are."

"Eat shit, Luis!"

"I can't help it if you're a wimp," Luis said. "I like cutting it close. It feels good."

"I'm not a wimp."

"Yeah, you are," Luis said. "And now that David is gone, you're the big wimp."

"Nice guy. David hasn't been gone ten minutes and you're already bad-mouthing him."

"I'd tell it to his face if he was standing right here."

"I wish he was here."

"I bet you he doesn't write," Luis said.

"Why do you say that?"

"You'll see."

"Bet you a tank of gas he does."

"You won't write either," Luis said.

"I could say the same thing about you," Carlos said.

"What do you mean?"

"You may leave before I do," Carlos pointed out.

Luis looked away to hide from Carlos his sudden sadness. He didn't want Carlos to figure out that he was lying about being able to leave Cuba, as he had told his friends.

From Amigos to Friends

Luis was saved by the bell when the orchestra started up, playing a hot cha-cha-cha that brought out to the outdoor dance floor several couples, including the big, dark *mulata* with the ham-size ass and coconut breasts that months ago had inspired Carlos to risk his life by diving off the Bottle. She wore a skimpy chocolate-shade bikini and red pumps that matched the color of the lipstick on her meaty lips. She kept blowing kisses to the musicians, which threw the whole orchestra off-key every time.

Drooling, Carlos said, "the only way I would stay in Cuba is if she married me."

"You wouldn't last two days. She'd chew you up and spit you out, dead."

"What a way to go," Carlos said, his head bouncing in rhythm with her firm buttocks.

Pelayo "Pete" Garcia

Sunday, October 15, 1961
Miami, Florida

Dear Carlos and Luis,

I wish you were here. You guys have to get out of Cuba as soon as you can. Everything in the United States is big. Even the people are big—including teenage girls! You have to see these girls to understand what I'm talking about. They're tall with long, beautiful legs and are as stacked as Laura's mother.

I'm living in a camp with thirty-one other Cuban guys. All of them have been here less than six months and they already have girlfriends. American girlfriends, because they go out on dates without chaperones. They like to kiss, and they don't talk as much as Cuban girls.

Last night they took us to the mall. You have to see this place to believe it! It's a giant shopping center with hundreds of stores under one roof. It's brand new. Everything here is new. If something doesn't work, you don't fix it, you throw it away. The stores are jam-packed with stuff. Even the walkways between stores are air-conditioned. I saw a store with televisions with really big screens, hi-fis with huge speakers, and more radios, TVs and record players than in all of Havana. Carlos, I went into a record store that has every record ever made, and not just one copy of each, but dozens. And best of all, no Cuban music. Luis, there's a bookstore so big you can't believe that so many books exist. I don't know why, but like a dummy, I was at first surprised that all the books were in English. I better work hard to improve my English. The guys at the camp say that the best way to get rid of the Spanish accent is to watch a lot of television and to get an American girlfriend. The TV makes sense, but the American girlfriend doesn't make any sense, since from overhearing the guys compare notes after their dates, it doesn't sound like they do a lot of talking.

This afternoon they took us to the beach. I wasn't planning to go in the water because it was freezing, but when we got there, all these Americans were in the water acting like it was the middle of summer, and all the other guys from the camp went in the water. I froze to death, but I didn't want to be the only wimp in the group. Since I'm the newest kid in the camp, I have to work twice as hard to earn everybody's respect.

This morning we went to Mass. So as you can see, it's not all fun around here.

For your mothers' sake, I hope to see your letters arriving soon.

Your best friend,
David

From Amigos to Friends

Sunday, October 15, 1961
Miami, Florida

Dear Mami and Papi,

I hope that when you receive this letter everything is well with you.

It's almost ten o'clock at night and because tomorrow is a school day, we have to be in bed before ten o'clock when they turn the lights out. So, don't blame me for this short letter.

I'm staying at a camp for boys who come out of Cuba by themselves. The oldest is eighteen and I'm the youngest.

The camp is run by two old Cuban couples. They are nice, but very strict. There are thirty-two guys in the camp. It's really two side-by-side houses.

Tomorrow I start school. They call it junior high school. I miss you a lot, but don't worry because I'll be okay until you get here. I love you very much.

Your son,
David

P.S. My address is on the back of the envelope.

CHAPTER XIII

David took to junior high school from day one. When David stepped out of his first period class on the first day of school in the United States, Tommy Jones, a very popular kid, approached David. "You're new here, aren't you?"

Insecure about his English, David kept his answer to a minimum. "Yes," he mumbled.

Tommy mistook David's self-doubt for an aloof edge that Tommy liked. "What's your name?" Tommy asked, flashing David a disarming smile.

"David." Out of habit, he said his name in Spanish. David cringed, hearing himself. He had practiced saying it in English for a whole hour the night before, but he'd just blown it.

Tommy made a face. "What?"

David took Tommy's reaction as a permanent rejection, and David moved away, disappointed with himself.

Among a rowdy crowd of students rushing up and down an open hallway to get to their next class, Tommy caught up with David. "You're okay," Tommy said. "I tell you what, I'll call you Danny."

David smiled and they shook hands. From that day on, David became David in Spanish and Danny in English. He didn't like it, but everyone else did.

It didn't take long for David to realize that getting good grades was not the popular thing to do in the United States. When he got a perfect grade in Geometry the first week of school, Tommy looked at him suspiciously and walked away. David recaptured the friendship by telling Tommy a story about copying the answers from the weird girl with glasses that sat next to him. Tommy felt better about David, but still could not understand why David had gone through all that trouble to get a good grade. Back in Cuba, David had always excelled in school. His parents' praise and encouragement had driven him to the top of his class, every year.

⚬⚬⚬

Back at camp, David began learning from his camp-mates everything worth knowing about becoming a success in the United States. It was all so simple. All he needed to do was to grow ten inches, gain seventy pounds, and learn to play football so he could make the high school team the following year. And, of course, he needed to buy a car. His roommates explained to him in expert detail that no girl could resist a Cuban football player who owned a car. And nothing in life compared with taking a different blonde every weekend to the drive-in theater.

David spent the afternoons after school in the back yard pumping iron. He stuffed himself at every meal until his stomach would threaten to blow up. After dinner, he played ping-pong. The game was a godsend, because even with all the weightlifting and gorging, he was still the scrawny one in camp. His quick reflexes and competitive drive made him a force to contend with at the ping-pong table.

He never did any homework. School seemed so easy. And, after all, why bother? He was on his way to a great future. But when the lights were turned off at the camp every night, in the solitude of his lower bunk, David feared the possibility of never seeing his parents again. The nightly sobbing heard through the house deepened his anxiety.

David fell asleep every night praying that his parents would arrive soon.

From Amigos to Friends

Sunday, December 3, 1961
Miami, Florida

Dear Mami and Papi,

I hope that when you receive this letter everything is well with you and my little brother. I'm fine.

I've grown an inch and gained five pounds since I arrived seven weeks ago. I'm now five-foot-three and weigh one-hundred-and-fifteen pounds. They feed us as much as we want. It's all American food: cold cereal with milk and sliced bananas for breakfast, hamburgers for lunch, and at dinner mostly steaks with mashed potatoes and vegetables. On Fridays they make us eat fish, but at school I still eat a hamburger for lunch. Every night we have ice cream for dessert.

We eat dinner at six and from seven to eight we do homework. Then from eight to ten we watch TV, or do whatever we want. I've been playing a lot of ping-pong. I'm ranked number two. Not bad, considering there are thirty-one other guys and they're all older than me.

Everything is fine at school. My English is getting better. I'm sure my grades will get better as my English improves.

It's getting really cold and it's been raining a lot. There's a rumor that the guys who have been here the longest will be shipped out to foster homes in different parts of the United States. We're staying inside a lot because of the rain. The feeling that they're going to break us up is putting everybody in a bad mood. I also think everybody is more homesick because Christmas is almost here.

I'll write you soon. I get your letters every week. They make me very happy and keep me from getting too homesick.

From your son who loves you and misses you,
David

Pelayo "Pete" Garcia

Sunday, December 3, 1961
Miami, Florida

Dear Carlos and Luis,

It's impossible to pay attention in class when my eyes are flying in every direction to check out the incredible female bodies all around the classroom. The best part about school here is called physical education, when the girls run around outside in very tight, short shorts.

Another thing that's really great about school here is that after every hour, you change classrooms. You get five minutes to go to the next classroom. Those five minutes are like one big party. Couples hold hands. I've even seen some kissing going on. Kids hang around in the hallways laughing, talking, flirting, making plans to meet at lunchtime or after school. Instead of going home and having a boring lunch with your parents, here you stay with your friends. If you saw me, you wouldn't recognize me. I've grown four inches and gained twenty pounds since I got here seven weeks ago. To really make it big in high school, I need to get a car. Without one you're nothing. With a car you take a date to the drive-in theater. They show the worst movies, but who cares, because you're in the back seat alone in the dark with a terrific-looking blonde with a body right out of a *Playboy* magazine centerfold and a face that, except for a few scattered pimples on her face, looks like a movie star. And there, in the privacy of your back seat, you make every daydream you've had in the shower come true.

I can get my driver's license in only thirteen-and-a-half months, when I turn sixteen. With some of the older guys here at the camp, I've been checking out the classified ads in the newspaper. You can buy a '54 Ford or Chevrolet in pretty decent shape for about three hundred dollars. The only problem is that before you're sixteen there aren't too many ways to make money. You need to be sixteen to get a work permit before you can get a regular job, like as a busboy at a restaurant, or pump gas at a gas station, or flip burgers at Burger King.

School is great. The classes are really easy. Everybody at school says I talk really well, that I have no accent, and that I don't even look Cuban, whatever that means. The classes are so easy, they're boring. I don't even take my books out of the locker. There are just too many good programs on TV to be bothering with homework. I'm also the camp's ping-pong champion.

Last Friday I went to a dance at the high school gym. My friend Tommy Jones and I sneaked in. It was incredible. The high school girls here have to be seen to be believed: tall, slender, super well built, and really friendly. I learned to do the "Twist." It's a new dance that's really popular. At the end of the dance, I had to walk back by myself because all the other guys from the camp who went ended up with a girl. I'm telling you, guys, fifteen more pounds and a couple more inches and I'm there. I can't wait for you guys to be here with me.

Well, I have to wrap it up because "Bonanza" starts in ten minutes.

Your best friend,
David

Back in Havana, Carlos and Luis would re-read David's letters until they had them memorized. They would meet every afternoon at Carlos' house after Luis got out of the public school he now attended. As the educator had predicted, all private schools had closed and Luis was now attending the public school on 10th Avenue and 96th Street.

Carlos was still out of school. His mother had insisted that he and his sister stay home until they left the country. She expected their exit papers any day. The wisdom in this was to avoid the educator's other prediction about the Revolution shipping kids out to Russia.

Staying at home alone took a toll on Carlos, especially since his father's presence became more and more mechanical by the day. Carlos sensed that his father was eager to have them leave as soon as possible. His mother's paranoia about losing her son and daughter to the Revolution before they had the opportunity to leave for the United States made getting permission to go out of the house practically impossible, forcing Carlos to escape out of the house through a window all the time. His mother would strip-search his sister, looking for hidden political propaganda every time she returned to the house after also escaping through a window.

After much screaming and yelling, and after Carlos threatened to join Fidel's militia if his mother didn't lighten her heavy hand, Carlos was allowed to ride his motorcycle and go to the beach with Luis on Saturdays.

Things with Silvia had been going really well. He was up to feeling her breasts under water at the beach, until one

Saturday she didn't show. The next day Carlos went by her house and found out she and her whole family had left for Miami.

—————

Luis continued to lead a double life. But as time passed, it became more difficult and complicated. With the closing of many churches and the exit from the island of most priests, Mrs. Rodríguez practically converted their house into a church. Votive candles burned twenty-four hours a day, turning black the ceiling above them. Statues of saints, from archangels to Lazarus, cluttered the living room—some statutes even sat on dining room chairs, giving the room a Last Supper look.

Several nights a week, ignoring her husband's warnings, Mrs. Rodríguez would have a dozen or so women friends at the house. Half of them dressed in black from head to toe. The praying of rosaries would last for hours and required complete silence, eliminating any chance of Luis listening to the radio or watching television. Some nights he even participated, rationalizing that it gave his mother so much satisfaction that it was worth having to walk like a cripple from sore knees the next day. How these old women could kneel for hours, day in and day out, was a mystery to him.

Luis drew the line when his mother suggested that he confess his sins weekly to one of the ladies in her rosary circle. This was necessary because priests were now scarce.

Luis' other life consisted of accompanying his father to Fidel's interminable speeches, in which the Maximum Leader, like an echo, repeated two or three times in a row every sentence that came out of his bearded mouth.

At school, Luis was pressured to join the Pioneros—the organization of students for the Revolution. After severe peer ʼessure and paternal manipulations, Luis became a full-ᵈ Pionero, complete with uniform, which was a junior version of his father's paratrooper uniform. Of course, he did so hidden from his mother. He would leave the house and return from school every day in his civilian clothes. A block from his house he would slip into a house that had stayed abandoned since its owners had left for Miami, and there he would change into the uniform he kept hidden there.

All during his rosary circle prayers, Luis begged God that his mother would never find him in uniform. Or even Carlos, for that matter.

The one advantage to his parents' lack of communication was that the whole thing would not come up in conversation.

CHAPTER XIV

On his fifteenth birthday, David fell in love with a girl in his English class. Her name was Claudia. She was five-foot-six, one-hundred-twenty pounds, and measured about 36-23-36. She had long, honey-colored hair, light green eyes, big white teeth, and was always tan, even though it was the middle of winter.

Claudia wore short dresses and sandals, which was good because she was a little taller than David. That didn't bother him too much because he was growing quickly. David figured that he would grow taller within a month or two. She wore her hair back in a ponytail and, except for a little lipstick, she didn't wear any makeup.

On a Monday five days before his birthday, Tommy Jones told David that Claudia had asked about David. Tommy's girlfriend had noticed that Claudia had become available because she wasn't wearing a ring on a chain around her neck. Claudia had asked her about "the cute guy in the light brown corduroy jacket." Everyone at the camp had received a great looking tan-colored corduroy jacket for Christmas from the Catholic Church.

Tommy, knowing that David drooled every time Claudia was any where near, immediately alerted David that Claudia had just broken up with her boyfriend. Tommy warned David he had to act fast and ask her out. She liked going steady, and being popular and good-looking, she wouldn't be available for long. It was good advice. David trusted Tommy in these matters. He was experienced. Although David knew he had to act fast, he chickened out that day. That night at camp, he consulted with some of the more experienced guys. They were seniors in high school. Their advice was simple: "Go for it! What do you have to lose?"

The next day, Tuesday, David went to school determined to ask Claudia for a date. There was no school dance that weekend, so going to the movies was his best bet. Money was his biggest concern. He needed a dollar fifty for each ticket, plus a dollar for a small popcorn and a Coke to share. He had gathered all this information from his counselors at camp. That Saturday he was counting on receiving the five-dollar birthday present the Catholic Church gave everyone. If he could work out the money issue, David knew going to the movies was ideal: dark, private, and no need for a car. He would take the bus to the mall and meet her there. He had it all worked out in his head. The next step was to ask her out.

That day she didn't show up for class. Absent! He was at first relieved, but then he turned into a bundle of nerves for the rest of the day.

On his way to school on Wednesday, he panicked, realizing he might not get his five-dollar birthday present until after his date on Saturday. And what would he do then for date money? She was at school that day, but he didn't dare ask her out without being absolutely certain that he would have the money in hand. Later in the day, David spotted Claudia talking to a lot of different guys. He became depressed, convinced that he had missed his chance. He feared that she would already have a date Saturday night. That night he arranged to borrow five dollars just in case. But it would be expensive, he would have to pay back the five bucks Sunday morning, plus a dollar a week in interest to a camp-mate who had a huge nose and claimed his father owned a bank in Cuba.

On Thursday, David made his move in front of her locker before their English class. "Hi, my name is Danny. Would you go to the movies with me Saturday night?" It came out perfect. Not a trace of an accent. He had practiced for hours and it had paid off.

She smiled back at him. He could tell she liked him. But then she said, "I can't. I already have a date."

David gave her that disappointed look Carlos had taught him, the one that worked so well with mothers, but not with fathers. "Oh no," he said, looking down at his shoes. "It's my birthday."

She thought for a second and then smiled. "I'll let you know tomorrow," she said. "Maybe I can break my date."

Hanging around Carlos' room on a rainy afternoon and listening to WFUN, Luis suddenly confessed to Carlos that he had joined the Pioneros. It was a hard confession for Luis to make, but he knew that Carlos would eventually find out, and Luis needed to confide his secret to someone. The pressure of leading a double life was taking a heavy toll on him.

"Why did you do that?" Carlos asked in disbelief.

"You wouldn't understand," Luis said, suddenly regretting having told Carlos.

"Try me. Make me understand."

"You would've done the same thing," Luis said.

"I don't think so, Luis. You're going to have to do better than that."

"There was a lot of pressure from the school and other kids."

"I would've said no."

"Easy for you to say," Luis said, defending himself, "just sitting on your ass here in your room all day."

"You think I like being stuck in the house all day?"

"That's not the point. Things are different. It's not like private school use to be. There's a lot of pressure in public school to belong, to be part of the Revolution. Why do you think your parents keep you at home?"

"Why didn't you tell your parents?"

"Carlos, if you tell your parents about this, I'll kill you. They would tell my mother, and she would have a nervous breakdown and die."

Luis proceeded to tell Carlos about the convoluted process he went through everyday to hide the Pionero uniform from his mother. The intrigue fascinated Carlos, prompting him to ask a multitude of "what if" questions about possible scenarios.

"You could've told your father," Carlos said, returning to the main issue. "He would've thought of something."

"My father?" Luis suddenly realized that he had painted himself into a corner and hoped that Carlos would miss the obvious.

"He more than anybody knows that joining the Pioneros is going to make it harder for you to leave the island," Carlos said.

"Carlos, that's why I had to join, don't you see?"

Carlos was now more confused than ever, but he was too vain to admit it. "I'm not sure I do."

"I've told you how my father's going to get us out, that his life is an act. To cover up that he's really against Fidel."

"What are you saying?" Carlos said. "That you becoming a Pionero is part of the act?"

"You know, Carlos," Luis said, thinking he'd pulled it off, "you're smarter than you look."

"And you know what, Luis?"

"What?"

"You're full of it. It's all a big lie. Your father is not against the Revolution."

"He is too."

"If it's all an act, then why is it you're so concerned that your mother finds out you've become a Pionero?"

172

Luis looked at his watch and stood up. "I got to go. It's too complicated. You just have to take my word for it."

Carlos got angry and, with one swift kick to the back of Luis' knees, brought his friend back to the floor. He grabbed Luis' arm and twisted it behind Luis' back until he screamed.

"Liar," Carlos said, twisting his friend's arm, sending Luis into severe pain. "You're going to tell me the truth or I'll break your arm."

"It's the truth," Luis protested, wincing with pain. "Let me go. You're breaking my arm."

Carlos twisted even more. "And if this doesn't work, I'll have Rocky rip your throat."

"Let go!" Luis screamed in pain.

"ROCKY!" Carlos screamed as if in pain. "ROCKY, HELP! LUIS IS HURTING ME!"

A thunderous bark suddenly shook the closed door of Carlos' room.

"ROCKY, HELP ME!"

The German shepherd pounded on the door, sending chills down Luis' back and flooding his brain with enough fear to block the pain of having his arm twisted out of its socket.

"Okay, okay, stop!" Luis begged. "Send Rocky away."

"Just kidding, Rocky!" Carlos' baby-talked to his dog, instantly calming the dog. "Stay right there, Rocky. In case Luis starts attacking me again."

Carlos warned Luis that even after he got his arm back, Luis had no choice but to spill it all out. The only way out of the room without telling Carlos the whole truth was over Rocky's dead body.

"It's all a lie, isn't it, Luis?"

Luis nursed his arm back into working order. He went out onto the balcony and decided he would break both legs if he jumped. It was definitely a superior alternative to confronting Rocky, but he decided that telling the truth was better. He would be found out eventually anyway. He sat back down on the floor and started his confession. "You're right. I made it all up. It's all a lie. My father is not against the Revolution. We're not leaving the country. I'm stuck here for the rest of my life," Luis said and his eyes watered. "I told you guys all that because I don't want to be the only one to stay back here. I'm afraid that I'll never see you and David ever again. You guys are my best friends. I don't have any other friends. I don't want other friends. If you go, I don't know what I'm going to do. Telling you guys that I was also leaving made me feel better. Believing my own lie made me feel better. Sometimes I think that if I say it and think it long enough, it will really happen." Luis put his face in his hands and broke down crying.

Carlos didn't know what to say or do. He had known Luis all his life and had never seen him cry. Luis had always been the toughest of the three, the one to push the limits. And when he fell on his ass, he just got right back up, dusting himself off as if nothing had happened. Carlos and David had assumed it had to do with how much fighting Luis' parents did at home. Luis had also told David and Carlos that he felt responsible for his family's problems.

"Maybe Fidel will fall and everything will go back to like before," Carlos said, not knowing what else to say.

"Yeah, right, sure."

"Or you can leave in a few years when you become an adult, like we talked about when David was here."

"That was a laugh," Luis said sarcastically.

"Why not?" Carlos insisted.

"Look, Carlos, I don't know how to explain it," Luis said. "My mother and father may or may not ever get back together again, but for some reason they can't be apart more than a few blocks, even if they don't talk to each other. I don't understand it, but that's the way they are. And I'm just like them. Since my father will never leave Cuba, we're all stuck here. It's not what I want, but that's the way it's going to be. Anything else would be another lie. I would do anything to make my parents get back together again. Anything. Sometimes I think that if I hadn't been born, they would be happy together."

"That's sick, Luis."

"It's true, they're always fighting over me..."

Carlos interrupted him. "Don't make yourself so important. My parents fight over me and my sister all the time. My sister says that if we weren't around, they would fight over something else."

"I'm going to miss you, Carlos."

"We'll always be best friends."

"You swear?"

"I swear."

Friday, after their English class, David met Claudia in front of her locker. His stomach kept doing somersaults, anticipating a rejection. He almost chickened out. Instead, he took a deep breath and went up to her. "Seven o'clock in front of the theater at the mall," he said confidently, following the advice of his experts back at the camp.

It worked. She liked it. She smiled. "Okay," she said. The bell rang. Kids ran to their classrooms all around them. They stood staring into each other's eyes. "We better go," she said, and they ran off in opposite directions.

Right away the word got out that David Oviedo was the reason why Claudia had broken her Saturday night date with Peter Brown, who happened to be the biggest guy in the entire junior high. He was so big, he practiced with the high school football team. All David heard at school the rest of the day was different versions of how Peter Brown was going to dismember him after Claudia revealed that she was dropping him for David. That day turned out to be truly one of David's luckiest. Not only had Claudia said yes, but Peter Brown had left school early to go practice with the high school football team.

David hardly slept Friday night. He stayed up very late talking to his advisors about his impending first date. They shared with him how their first dates had turned out, and what, in retrospect, they would have done differently.

Saturday morning he got up early and pumped iron out in the back yard. After lunch, he took a long shower, put on lots of deodorant, and shaved. Nothing came off, but his face felt very smooth. He took an early bus to the mall and arrived an hour early. He bought two tickets for the seven o'clock show and waited. At a quarter past seven, he resigned himself to a life of failure and rejection. And then he saw her. She came running with her long, blonde ponytail flopping behind her. They rushed inside and sat in the back row of the nearly empty theater. The movie was in progress. He went out and returned with a small popcorn and a small Coke to share. They ate in silence. He couldn't take his eyes off her, but acted like he was interested in the movie.

Claudia asked him how old he was.

"Sixteen," he lied, adding a year to his age.

He slipped his hand over hers. She turned her hand, their palms touched, and their fingers interlocked. He held her hand, firmly. He kept checking from the corner of his eye for any signal that the time was right to kiss her. She seemed completely involved with the movie. He became concerned. Suddenly, she rested the back of her neck against the backrest. She turned toward him. Her big green eyes traveled his face until their eyes locked. Her lips parted, moist and shiny. She closed her eyes as his lips reached for hers. Their lips touched, and he felt her small, soft tongue searching for his.

The advice from his buddies from camp worked. "You're a good kisser," she said after their long, passionate kiss. "Happy birthday."

From Amigos to Friends

David wondered what she would think if he told her that he had just kissed a girl for the first time in his life. They kissed through a double feature and several cartoons. He caressed her face, her neck, her shoulders, her arms, her thighs. Her body was firm. Her skin was warm. They hugged. She kissed his neck, his ear. It drove him crazy.

He knew he wanted to go steady with her, but didn't have a ring to give her. He kicked himself for not being prepared. Sure, he didn't have the money, but he could've made one out of a big nut at the school's wood shop, like Tommy Jones had done. He considered asking her to go steady and promising her the ring on Monday, but decided against it. He concluded that she deserved better than that. He was confident that after the way they had kissed, he could stall for a couple of days.

On Sunday morning, he borrowed five dollars from Big Nose, and that afternoon he walked five miles to the mall. It didn't seem that far because he thought about Claudia the entire way, recounting how it had felt to hold her in his arms, to have her lips pressed against his neck. The five dollars had not afforded a lot of choice, but the ring was presentable—simple, but elegant. And with the two cents per paper he was going to start making, selling newspapers at a traffic light on Monday, he could pay off Big Nose and soon afford a more substantial ring for Claudia.

He was in love. She was everything he could ask for. Beautiful, smart, a great dresser, and so popular. I'm so lucky she likes me, he thought.

Everything was going great, except for the disastrous report card he had received on Friday. And then on Sunday morning, a black cloud settled over the entire camp when Raúl, David's bunk-mate, received word that his father had been arrested in Cuba and had been promptly executed by a firing squad. Raúl, like David and everyone else at the camp,

Pelayo "Pete" Garcia

had been momentarily expecting his parents' arrival in the United States.

Sunday, January 14, 1962
Miami, Florida

Dear Mami and Papi,

I hope that when you receive this letter everything is well with you. Today, I got the letter you wrote before Christmas.

Papi, I'm sorry that you're concerned about my schoolwork. I think that you shouldn't worry about it. I had nothing to do with getting a light school load. On the first day of school, I was sent to a counselor who asked me a couple of questions and then gave me that schedule. I pointed out to him that I had already taken Algebra in Cuba. He must've assumed that Algebra was a lot easier in Cuba and that it would be good for me to repeat it. I wasn't very confident about my English, so I didn't argue with him. I was afraid that I would speak badly and he would put me back a year in the eighth grade.

I haven't received a report card. I don't think here in the United States they give report cards until the end of the year. I've been looking for ways to make some money so I can buy a family car for when you get here. A lot of the guys here sell newspapers after school. It only takes an hour a day and two hours on Saturday. That'll leave me with plenty of time to do my homework. I can save enough money so when you get here we can have a car. Everything here is far away. Without a car you can't do anything.

I can't wait for you to get here.

Your son who loves you and misses you,
David

From Amigos to Friends

Wanting to see Luis wearing his Pionero uniform, Carlos climbed out of his living room window and walked the ten blocks to the public school. In front of a snow cone vendor's pushcart, Carlos waited for school to let out. He bought a coconut flavored snow cone and wished he could go back to school. He hated school, but staying home with his mother, his sister, and the maid all day long was starting to make him think like a woman.

School let out and a good percentage of the boys wore the Pionero uniform, as Luis had claimed. It looked like an army of midgets, Carlos thought. Carlos got distracted flirting with a group of girls now surrounding the snow cone vendor, and he dripped coconut syrup all over his shirt. The girls giggled. I haven't lost my touch, Carlos thought.

Luis appeared looking like a pint-size version of his father and insisted that Carlos buy him a cone. Carlos refused, and Luis threatened to expose him as a counterrevolutionary worm to a group of Pioneros hanging around the front of the school. Carlos decided that dispensing with the extra nickel he had in his pocket was worth not finding out if Luis was serious or not.

Slurping their snow cones, they headed for the abandoned house where Luis kept the regular clothes he wore to and from his house. The plan was for Luis to show Carlos the whole routine of a double life, like spies in movies. Carlos kept teasing Luis about looking just like his father, if he only moved the hair on top of his head over to cover his face.

Distracted with their cones and their conversation, Luis' worst nightmare took them by surprise. Reaching the abandoned house, they failed to notice Luis' mother coming out of a house across the street, carrying the sewing and embroidery kit she took to her clients' houses. At first Mrs. Fernández only recognized Carlos and called out his name to say hello.

Pelayo "Pete" Garcia

Hearing his mother's voice, Luis became paralyzed. The cone slipped out of his hand, splattering on the sidewalk. Carlos took off running.

Realizing that the boy dressed in one of those despicable Pionero uniforms was her one and only son Luis, Mrs. Rodríguez let out a primal scream that curled Luis' blood and froze Carlos in mid-stride.

Carlos stayed with Luis and his mother during the three blocks of forced march back to Luis' house. Every step was torture, not because of anything said, since Mrs. Rodríguez remained completely silent after the primal scream, but because the silence only heightened the fear of events to come. Carlos abandoned Luis as they reached the front of Carlos' house. With one cowardly sprint, Carlos disappeared inside his house, went outside again through the back door, and hid under the window ledge of Luis' living room. He helped himself to a front row seat for the fight of the century.

A half-hour later, Mr. Rodríguez arrived. He had been summoned by telephone to report within thirty minutes, under the threat of Mrs. Rodríguez committing suicide. Luis sat meekly on a chair, displaying the guilt and remorse of someone caught in the act of committing a violent crime.

"What's the big deal?" Mr. Rodríguez said, dismissing the whole thing as he sat down on the sofa.

"That's exactly what the problem is," Mrs. Rodríguez fired back. "You are too irresponsible to even understand the gravity of the problem."

Mr. Rodríguez sprang up from the sofa and said, "Let's get one thing straight right now. One more insult from you and I'll leave. After that I don't care what you do to yourself."

Luis panicked. He wanted to say something, but the words would not come out of his mouth.

Mrs. Rodríguez jumped out of her seat and went nose-to-nose with her estranged husband. "That's really what's behind all this. I've known it all along. You just want to get rid of me.

You want me dead. You want me out of the way so you can start a new life. Why don't you tell the whole truth? You don't want your children either. You don't want any of us. The only important thing to you is this stupid Revolution! Go ahead, tell your son the truth. You don't care about me. You don't care about him. All you care about is Fidel."

Mr. Rodríguez became alarmed by her fury and sat down again on the sofa. He was speechless.

Luis broke down crying.

Mrs. Rodríguez continued venting her rage. "You knew that getting your son in that idiotic Pionero band of fanatics would kill me. But you forced Luis to join. That proves my point. What is it? You have another woman. Or two. Or three, now that you're a big shot. A big Communist that goes around stealing other people's things. You'll burn in hell for all of this! God is watching you. You'll pay!"

"Mami, Papi didn't force me to join the Pioneros," Luis said in a quivering voice.

Mrs. Rodríguez continued her relentless verbal punishment. "You have corrupted your son. He wants to imitate you, even if it kills his own mother. Now he wants to become evil, just like you. How could you do this? How could you turn my own son against me like this?"

"Mami, please," Luis begged his mother. "It's nothing like that. I just wanted to fit in at my new school. It's nothing against you. I love you, Mami."

His mother turned on her heels and now towered over Luis. "You lied to me. You deceived your mother. You sneaked around and did what you knew would hurt your mother. Is that how you love me, Luis? Is that how you show your love for your mother? By worshipping a false Revolution like your father does? Is that how you love your mother, son?"

Mr. Rodríguez finally spoke. He spoke softly and without a trace of animosity. "I wish I knew what to say to assure you that I still love you... to assure you that we are not doing anything to try to harm you. You are the only woman in my life. Your son worships you..."

"I do, Mami," Luis said, interrupting his father.

Mr. Rodríguez continued, and his wife sat down. "Life in this country has changed and it will continue to change. The old ways are gone. That's why it's called a Revolution. The ones who don't like it leave the island. The rest of us, like you, need to change, need to accept the changes and stop fighting them. If not, you'll make us all crazy. We're killing each other over things that are the way things are going to be like from now on. The Pioneros is an organization that gives kids a place to experience the Revolution. It's not an evil thing. Luis joined because all the kids who are not staying at home, because they are leaving like Carlos next door, are part of it. He's just becoming part of the whole. Do you want Luis to become a misfit? An outsider in his own country?"

"Is that right, Luis?" Mrs. Rodríguez asked her son. "Is your father accurate in what he's saying? Do you want to be like him? To abandon Christian values and join the Revolution?"

Luis hesitated. He wasn't sure where his mother was headed with all these questions. "Mami, I just want to belong. Since we're staying in Cuba, I have to be part of the whole, like Papi just said."

His mother slowly stood up and said firmly, "You have made your choice, Luis. And I won't stand in your way. But I also will not be part of it. I want you to immediately pack your things and go live with your father. Good luck, son." She turned around and disappeared inside her bedroom.

An hour later, Luis moved out of his mother's house. With a small duffle bag tied to the back of his motorcycle, he rode off tailing his father's motorcycle. Carlos waved until they banked the curb and Luis disappeared. Carlos and Luis had hugged, but had not shared a word. They knew not what to say.

From Amigos to Friends

Monday morning, David took an early bus and arrived at the junior high an hour early. He didn't mind, it gave him more time to rehearse showing her the ring and proposing that she go steady with him. He immediately recognized her parents' Cadillac when it pulled up in front of the school. She got out of the car and rushed toward her locker. He couldn't believe it, she was even more attractive than in his fantasies.

In front of her locker, David suddenly froze. A huge ring hung from her neck.

She looked up and realized he was staring at the ring around her neck. "Hi," she said as if they had never kissed.

Speechless, David just stared at the ring around her neck.

"I'm going steady with Peter Brown," she said, holding the ring up for David to admire. "Isn't it great?"

"Since when?" David asked, finally finding his voice.

"Last night."

"Didn't our date mean anything?"

"It was nice."

"I thought..."

She interrupted him. "I like going steady. You didn't ask me, so I moved on."

"Moved on?"

The bell rang. Claudia closed her locker and sauntered away.

David stood in place, immobilized. Kids ran in all directions around him.

That night, lying in bed feeling sorry for himself after skipping dinner, David opened a letter from his parents that had arrived that afternoon. In the past, he had immediately read their letters, but after the incident with Claudia he was

not fit to receive anymore bad news. The news was always the
same: Even though his parents were not able to join him just
yet, they were hopeful that their reunion would come soon.

Thursday, January 8, 1962
Havana, Cuba

Dear David,

We leave for Miami in fourteen days. Tuesday, January 22, 1962. It's
going to be the happiest day of my life. Your father just walked in the door
with the exit permits. What a surprise! We were losing hope, and then two
days ago the man your father had dealt with returned from Moscow and
everything fell into place.

The man walked into the store twenty minutes ago and shocked your
father when he handed him the documents. Your father immediately closed
the store and rushed home. I've never seen such a big smile on your father's
face, ever since I said yes when he proposed to me. I gave him a huge kiss,
and I immediately sat down to write to you. All of us can't wait to see you, to
be with you, to hear what you've been doing beyond the bits and pieces of
information we get from your letters.

Our separation has been hard on all of us. Now that we're going to be
together soon, I can tell you how sad it's been, how lonely it's been, how much
we've missed you. Few hours ever go by without a conversation about you, or
a memory that brings tears to my eyes. I know you'll cringe at these words,
but to me you'll always be that warm bundle I rocked to sleep so many nights.

Your brother has been very depressed. He's a very sensitive boy and, of
course, he hasn't learned to hide his feelings like us adults. He's so good-
natured. A week ago we had a little party for his third birthday. All the
neighbors chipped in and we gathered enough flour, eggs, butter, and chocolate to bake your brother a small birthday cake. As your father lit the third
and last candle, Margarita from across the street ran in through the kitchen
door with the news that the grocery store on Fifth avenue and Ninety-second
Street had just received a shipment of coffee and soap. The birthday song
came to an abrupt stop, and all the neighbors rushed out of the house, leaving
your father, your poor brother, and me silently staring at the candles melting
down on your brother's birthday cake. Your brother deserves better than that.

I'm so happy that we're going to be together again and that we're going
to start a new life that will give you and your brother every opportunity possible to pursue a bright future, so that both of you can become and achieve
whatever you choose.

I wish we were leaving this very moment. I love you.

Mami

From Amigos to Friends

Dear Son,

Today, everything appears different. It feels new and exciting. It's a new beginning. It scares me. Your father is not a young man anymore. I'm forty-one-years old, with probably half my life now behind me. For a long time I've resented the uncharted future destiny is dealing us. Why couldn't life stay as it once was: simple, comfortable, predictable? I've been scared to leave everything behind.

Now I'm excited to start over again. I'm mature enough to know that this euphoria will pass and the doubts and fears will return, but I know that we're a strong, tight-knit family and that together we'll overcome all obstacles.

Your absence has confirmed to me that being together as a family justifies any effort, any hardship, any sacrifice required. No material object, no creature comfort is important if not shared with the ones we love, or if they prevent an individual from reaching his or her full potential, or interfere with our morals and ethics.

It won't be easy, but we'll do it together.

I'm also glad that I will see you soon, because from the pack of lies and excuses in your letters about your dismal results at school, it's obvious you desperately need your parents' supervision.

I can't wait to be with you. I love you.

Papi

David read the letter over and over. Yes! Yes! It was in only two days. His mother, father, and brother were arriving on the one daily flight from Cuba: Pan American Airlines landing at 10:25 a.m. It was the same flight he had taken a few months back. He read the letter three times and then twice more.

He decided to keep the news to himself and turned off his reading light. He tossed and turned all night long.

The Saturday after Luis' mother had thrown Luis out of the house, Carlos and Luis had agreed on the phone to spend the day at the beach. Carlos had suggested going to the movies, but Luis had insisted on going to the beach. Carlos had protested, pointing out that the middle of January was not the best time to go swimming, even if the weather had not been particularly cold. Luis had insisted and Carlos had relented when he considered what Luis was going through. They had agreed to meet at the Bottle at eleven in the morning.

Carlos had spent the morning out in the front yard playing with Rocky and thinking of the best way to tell Luis that David's parents had received their exit papers and were leaving in the next few days. Carlos knew that Luis would take it hard because it would resurface all the emotions over David's departure.

A government official arrived on a motorcycle and confirmed with Carlos that he was at the right address. The messenger then marched up to the front door where Carlos' mother signed for the package. There was no doubt what had just arrived, sending violent mixed emotions up Carlos' spine: joy knowing that his exit papers had just arrived and he was only days away from arriving in the United States and seeing David, but terror at the thought of the effect it would have on Luis. And of course he felt bad about leaving Rocky behind.

From Amigos to Friends

All the way to the beach on his motorcycle, Carlos debated whether or not to tell Luis that he was leaving for Miami in a week. He had considered not showing up and later telling Luis from the safety of his balcony that he was very sick and had to skip the beach. That way, he would gain enough time to figure out what to do. He scrapped that plan, concluding that his mother was already on the phone calling and telling all her friends, and shortly Luis' mother would hear it from some gossiping neighbor. Luis was very strict about these things and would never forgive Carlos for not telling him. There's no alternative, Carlos thought. I have to tell him.

When Carlos arrived wearing his swimming trunks and a T-shirt, he was surprised that the beach was packed, considering it was the middle of January. As always, the orchestra was on stage, playing a blistering *merengue* that had the crowd in a sweat, even the ones not dancing. Luis was nowhere in sight. Carlos went over to the small, circular dance floor in front of the orchestra and became hypnotized by the sensual rhythm of round, dark, meaty hips swaying to the rapid beat of the spicy *merengue*. Some things he was going to miss about Cuba.

Suddenly, his swimming trunks flew off his hips and ended up around his ankles. Behind him, Luis screamed, turning every head in Carlos' direction. Carlos immediately bent over and quickly slipped his trunks back on. All sorts of loud, lewd comments, whistles, and catcalls followed.

Carlos chased Luis all the way to the thatch-roofed bar on the sand near the water's edge. "Even your buns turned red," Luis said, laughing his head off.

"You're a jerk, Luis. No wonder your mother threw you out."

Luis' laughter came to a sudden stop. "Eat shit, Carlos," Luis said, climbed on a stool, and ordered an Hatuey beer.

Carlos took the stool next to Luis and ordered a lemonade.

Luis scoffed at Carlos. "When are you going to stop being a sissy and start drinking beer like a man?" Luis said.

"You're a turd, Luis. Do you think drinking beer is going to make a man out of you. You're not even fifteen yet."

"It's not how old you are," Luis said, full of himself, "but what you carry between your legs."

Carlos almost fell out of his stool laughing.

The bottle of beer arrived and Luis guzzled it down, as if to prove a point. "Hey, bartender, two more Hatueys. One for me and one for my friend here," Luis said. "Come on, Carlos, your mother is nowhere around. Don't be such a mama's boy. Live a little."

The two beers arrived and Carlos succumbed to Luis' pressure. Carlos sipped his while Luis took big gulps. Carlos had snuck a few out of the refrigerator back home, but had not yet "developed a taste for it," as Luis had told him—it had been the same with cigarettes.

Carlos decided to test Luis' emotional waters and started out asking him how things were going living with his father. Luis was putting on a good show, declaring that he was much better off not having to lead a double life. He said he was ready to become a man, and being out from under his mother's apron was best for him. Luis kept guzzling down beer as if to numb his feelings.

Carlos then eased into telling Luis about David's parents receiving their exit papers and leaving for Miami within a few days. Luis came back with more logical rationalizations as to why it was for the best, since David's parents were going to leave eventually anyway.

It wasn't until Luis had downed six beers to Carlos' three that Carlos dropped the big bomb. It wasn't planned, it just slipped out as Carlos became distracted when Luis opened his last bottle of beer with his teeth.

"Shit, Luis, I'm really going to miss you," Carlos said laughing. Five seconds later, after his own words had slowly entered his ears and his numbed brain had slowly processed the words, his face turned as white as the sand at his feet.

Luis would have had to be blind, deaf, and dumb not to notice all the panic symptoms registered all over Carlos. "When?" Luis simply asked as if he had become instantly sober.

"When what?" Carlos asked back, making a complete fool of himself.

"Don't be an asshole, Carlos. When do you leave for Miami?"

"A week," Carlos said sheepishly and felt an instant urge to pee from the effect of the three beers. He also felt an urge to dig a hole and disappear.

Luis turned his back to Carlos and ordered another beer. Carlos didn't know what to say. What could he say? There was really nothing to say. They sat in silence, Carlos staring at Luis' back until the beer arrived and Luis guzzled it down. The sound of the beer going down drove Carlos' bladder to the red zone. He jumped out of his stool and ran to the men's room.

When he returned from the bathroom, no more than five minutes later, Luis was gone. Carlos looked all around, but did not spot his best friend. He asked the bartender and was told that Luis had paid and had weaved toward the water. A chill shook Carlos when he gazed toward the ocean and spotted Luis swimming toward the Bottle. Carlos yelled Luis' name at the top of his lungs and in a panic ran toward the water. He hit the water running and swam as fast as he could.

Luis reached the top of the Bottle, teetering. He stood on the two-foot diameter top, and looked down at the concrete platform twenty feet below and at the water ten feet beyond.

Carlos swam to the ladder and began quickly climbing up to the concrete platform. "Luis, please get down from there!" Carlos begged. As Carlos reached the platform, he saw Luis lose his footing and, then with complete abandonment, Luis threw himself headfirst through the air.

At the hospital, Carlos was put under heavy sedatives after Luis was pronounced dead. Carlos had kept volunteering to the police, over and over, how it had been an accident.

◆━━◆━━◆

The day of his parents' announced arrival, David was up before dawn. He showered, shaved, skipped school, and hitched a ride to the airport.

Two hours before the plane's arrival, David reached the area where the passengers exited the immigration office. The place was already packed with anticipating relatives and friends. They stood behind a waist-high chainlink fence lining the dark glass double doors leading out of the immigration area. It was a frantic, anxious crowd, noisier than the already loud reputation his compatriots were known for.

Why all Cuban women cried incessantly at moments like these, he never understood. In contrast, the men argued politics, trying to be more anti-Castro than anyone. The children spoke to each other in English, and the teenagers flirted with one another. The announcement of the arrival of the flight over the intercom sent the crowd into a frenzy, and it sent chills up and down David's spine.

When the first person, an elderly woman, cautiously stepped outside the double doors, David heard a primal "MAMA! MAMA! MAMA!" above the collective outburst of raw emotions emanating from the crowd. The old woman nervously squinted, slowly stepped forward, and then melted in the arms of her sixty-year-old child. Father Michael came out next, shepherding two girls and a boy. After a half-hour, David felt exhausted as, one by one, the passengers from his parents' flight stepped into the arms of friends and relatives. He panicked when five minutes passed without anyone else coming out of the building.

Alone now, he started hyperventilating. He gripped the chainlink fence with both hands. An immigration officer stepped out through the double doors and went to David. "I'm sorry, son. Everyone that came in on that plane has left."

David couldn't find his voice.

"It happens all the time," the man said, sympathetically. "They change passengers at the last minute down there."

David refused to break down.

"Is it your parents?" the man asked.

David barely nodded.

"They'll probably be out in the next few days," the man said, placing his hand on David's shoulder. "It happens sometimes, son."

CHAPTER XV

On his return to the camp after leaving the airport, David changed buses twice. Arriving at the camp, he realized he did not remember anything about the three hours spent getting back. His mind had gone blank, returning via automatic pilot.

Will I ever see my parents again? Are they alive? Why didn't they show? There was no one to ask, no one to go to. Everyone at the camp had their own problems, their own crosses to bear.

Commenting on what had happened would only lead to the telling by others at the camp of their own horror stories about relatives or friends.

After skipping dinner and finding solace in his lower bunk facing a white wall in the dark, David decided that if he was going to be without his parents, possibly forever, it was time for some changes.

I'm not going to be dependent on anybody or anything. And I'm going to get out of this stupid camp. I'm getting a car, too—no more three-hour bus trips. No more mister nice guy with the likes of Claudia. I'm going to be my own man.

The first deed in his self-proclaimed emancipation was to disregard his father's school demands by cutting all his afternoon classes the next day. A few blocks away from the school he stole a bicycle left alone in a front yard. A few hours later, he and his new bicycle were hired by the *Miami Herald* to deliver the morning paper—a paper route with one-hundred-and-twenty papers. And an hour later, he was selling the

Miami News afternoon paper at a traffic light. If he was going to be alone in the United States, he needed money. And money he would get—as much and as fast as possible, one way or another. To crown his new independence, he promised himself a car. He knew full well that having just turned fifteen left him a full year from being able to get a driver's license. I'll figure something out, he thought, counting on his friend Tommy for advice, suspecting that his American friend was not yet sixteen and somehow drove his own car, a great looking '57 Chevy convertible with four-on-the-floor and leather interior.

And Tommy indeed had a way. It was even simpler than David had imagined, but more expensive than he had counted on. The secret was called a fake ID, and Tommy could get him a fake driver's license for thirty dollars.

"Thirty dollars!" David complained.

"Do you want to drive, or do you want to ride the bus one more year?" Tommy pointed out.

"Even with the paper route and selling papers at the corner, it's going to take me forever to save three hundred bucks to buy a car, and now thirty more for the license," David complained again.

"Don't knock it," Tommy said. "You can make good money with that paper route."

"Yeah, right," David said, totally frustrated.

"Hey, man, I'm telling you," Tommy continued, "that's how I make all my dough."

David checked out Tommy's expensive loafers, buttoned-down Madras shirt and matching belt, and then his cherry '57 Chevy behind him. David skeptically asked, "You have a paper route?"

Tommy almost died laughing. When he recovered, he let David in on his secret to success. "Let's just say that my associates have paper routes that make us tons of money."

"Associates?"

"Yeah, associates," Tommy said, full of himself.

"Can I become an associate?" David asked, looking over Tommy's shoulder at the red leather interior of his friend's Chevy.

"Maybe," Tommy said, playing hard to get.

"What kind of paper routes do they have?" David asked. "They must be huge."

"Yours will work," Tommy said with confidence.

"It's only one-hundred-twenty papers," David pointed out.

"No problem."

"How many papers do you help me with?" David said, assuming that Tommy with his car would do part of the work.

"No, no, you deliver the papers," Tommy said.

David smiled, figuring out that Tommy had been pulling his leg all along. Tommy was known to pull practical jokes all the time, and he especially liked to work David over because sometimes David didn't pick up the language subtleties or the slang. David decided to play along, to see how far Tommy would go, and to try to trip up his friend and turn the joke around on him.

"Okay, let's do it," David said. "I'll become your associate. How much do I make then?"

"You get a third. That's a damn good deal," Tommy said. "Only because we're buddies."

"That's great!" David said. "I do all the work and you get two-thirds."

"You can probably make three hundred bucks and buy your car in a month," Tommy said.

Greed seeped in through every pour in David's skin. "Three hundred bucks in a month? I can have a car in a month?" David couldn't take his eyes away from Tommy's wire wheel hubcaps.

"Yeah, and you don't have to go in. I do that," Tommy said.

"Go in?" David asked suspiciously.

"Yeah, two scores in a month and we stop," Tommy said. "It gets too suspicious after that."

"What are you talking about?" David asked, totally confused at that point.

"It's a piece of cake." Tommy began to explain the whole scheme to David. "You'll know when someone goes out of town. Like on vacation and stuff. They'll tell you so you don't deliver papers that lay around saying, 'Hey, nobody here... come on in and rob us.' You find out they're splitting and then you like go collect when they're not home and find out where they hid a key. It's dumb. They always hide a key or leave a window partly open to let the cat in. It's not suspicious. You're the paperboy. One night I go in and clean up. TV, radio, cash, jewelry, clothes, the works. Piece of cake. I got a buddy that fences it all for me. We get the dough in a week. I average five hundred a pop. That's over one-fifty for you."

David was speechless.

"Easy money, David," Tommy said. "Like taking candy from a baby."

"What if you get caught?"

"That's my problem, isn't it?"

"You wouldn't tell about me?"

"Even if I did, you think they're going to believe me. You're just a paperboy, for Christ sake."

"I don't know," David said. "I have to think about it."

Tommy got in his detailed '57 Chevy and turned the engine over. "Let me know when you're ready, partner." Tommy winked and the Chevy burned rubber.

━━━

When the mailman arrived at the camp early Saturday afternoon, David was in the back yard pumping iron. All the eating, vitamins and training with weights was finally paying off, now that his growth hormones were kicking into high gear. He was almost five-foot-nine and one-hundred-forty pounds of lean muscle.

David heard his name being called out, learning that he had received mail, but he continued his workout. Later that afternoon, Tommy was going to pick him up in his Chevy convertible to go out together on a double date. This was David's second date. He was excited and nervous. He hardly knew this girl. He had seen her at school, but had hardly said two words to her. She was one of the best looking and most popular girls in the school. She was definitely his type: tall, blonde, and with great legs and big tits.

David thought of what a great friend he had in Tommy, who had arranged the date for him and was going to let David and his date use the back seat at the drive-in theater they were going to that night.

Tommy was going to pick him up early so he and Tommy could go eat a Whopper and a milk shake at the Burger King before picking up their dates. But before that, Tommy wanted to drive through David's paper route. David had not agreed to become Tommy's associate, but he was certainly thinking about it.

Pelayo "Pete" Garcia

Tuesday, January 14, 1962
Havana, Cuba

Dear David,

We've just returned from the airport, where we were taken off the airplane at the last minute. We're safely at home. They did not detain us, but simply sent us home without an explanation.

The government official whom I spoke to you about, and who has been helping us expedite our papers, is trying to find out what happened. He doesn't think it has anything to do with my previous arrest during the invasion. He says it was probably an error and that we should be able to leave soon. Unfortunately, it may take a few days to find out what happened.

We hope to be with you soon. Your mother, of course, is extremely upset.

David, Carlos is due to arrive in Miami with his mother and sister in the next few days.

I regret having to tell you that Luis died two days ago. I was going to tell you in person, knowing how hard you will take this news. It's been very painful for everyone here. Mrs. Rodríguez has been hospitalized, suffering from a nervous breakdown. Luis died from head injuries sustained from an accident diving off the Bottle at the public beach.

I wish I could be with you to help you with the loss of your friend. Dr. Blanco, a psychiatrist friend of your mother's, has advised me that it would be good for you to talk to someone about your feelings and not to bottle them up. Anyone would do—a priest, a friend, a girlfriend, anyone.

Please don't despair over our delay. My contact assures me that our exit will be prompt. I'll let you know as soon as I find out what's going on.

Your mother, your brother, and I miss you terribly, and we're sure we'll be with you in the very near future.

Love,
Papi

From Amigos to Friends

David stuck his head and then the rest of his body under a torrent of hot water, and then he stood immobilized for a long time under the shower, his mind spinning. Luis is dead? Luis is dead? Luis is dead? Luis is dead? The question echoed over and over again in his mind. "Luis died from head injuries sustained from an accident diving off the Bottle at the public beach." "Luis died from head injuries sustained from an accident diving off the Bottle at the public beach." "Luis died from head injuries sustained from an accident diving off the Bottle at the public beach." "Luis died of head injuries sustained from an accident diving off the Bottle at the public beach."

He pressed his ears hard with both hands, trying to end the tormenting echo. He concentrated on Carlos' arrival, trying to ease his pain, but only succeeded in wondering if Carlos had been there with Luis. He thought back to the days the three of them had gone to the public beach. Luis had been the fearless one, the first one to fly past the concrete deck and safely reach the waters below. He thought of his own fears and how close he himself had come to hitting the concrete. David's legs almost gave out from under him in the shower. He was sure Carlos had been there. Was it an accident? Was it an accident? Was it an accident? Was it an accident? echoed in his brain. It wasn't a question he consciously asked himself, but a question asked against his own will.

Someone pounded on the bathroom door and loudly threatened his life if David used all the hot water. David yelled back for whomever it was banging on the door to go to hell. David then thought of his parents and he gave thanks for their well-being, finally able to confirm, what he had assumed all along, that his parents and kid brother were not in danger, but that their departure from Cuba would be slow in coming, if at all.

Shaved and wearing a black shirt and pants and a brand new pair of black boots, just like the ones Tommy always wore, David sat on the front porch of the camp-house waiting for Tommy to arrive in his convertible. He had bought the boots that morning with the money he had made the first week delivering the *Herald* every day at five in the morning and selling the *News* at three in the afternoon at the traffic light on the intersection of Northwest 79th Street and 27th Avenue. A nickel a paper, Monday through Friday, every afternoon. At two cents a paper take-home money, it had required peddling a lot of papers and many close calls with speeding cars. The thirteen dollars, plus sales tax, for the boots had wiped out all the money David had made that first week, so he was borrowing five dollars from Tommy to pay for his date.

David noticed a skinny kid a block down the street, rushing down the sidewalk headed in David's direction. The kid then yelled out David's name. At first David couldn't believe his eyes. It was Carlos. David jumped out of his chair and yelled out Carlos' name. They met on the sidewalk in front of the camp. They hugged and screamed in joy. Carlos was a good four inches shorter, twenty pounds less, and his eyes had dark circles under them, as if Carlos hadn't slept in a week. Back in Cuba they had been the same size.

"I just found out you were arriving," David said. "I read it an hour ago. And here you are."

"David, it's so great to see you," Carlos said. "I've been daydreaming about this moment since the day you left."

"When did you get here?"

"Two days ago. We stayed with a family that took us in until we found a place to live. This morning we moved in to our new place. It's a shoebox, but you won't believe this. It's ten blocks from here. We're neighbors again!"

"That's great! That means we'll be going to school together," David said. "We'll see each other every day!"

"Hey, how did you get so big?" Carlos asked.

"You'll get big, too," David assured his friend. "Something about the food here."

"This is so great," Carlos said. "It's just like before."

David lowered his chin and stared at his new boots. Carlos immediately knew what David was thinking. It took a while for the conversation to reactivate. Neither one of them knowing how to deal with the subject of losing their best friend.

"My father wrote me what happened," David finally broke the silence.

Carlos became very upset, almost shaking. "What did he say?"

"You know. About Luis' accident," David said, staring at his boots. "That he died."

"I can't talk about it, David," Carlos said, shaking. "The doctors said I have to wait a while before I start dealing with it. I'm taking this medicine that's helping."

They both realized that the other had tears running down his face.

"Fine with me," David said. "I don't even want to know what happened. I don't even want to believe it. As far as I'm concerned, nothing happened."

"Let's go to my house," Carlos said, changing the subject. "We can talk all night long about everything else."

"I don't know, Carlos," David said. "Tonight is a bad night."

"A bad night?" Carlos asked.

At that moment Tommy's '57 Chevy convertible, with the top down, pulled up to the curb.

Tommy pulled himself up from behind the steering wheel and sat up on the back rest of the front seat and planted his ever-present black boots on the steering wheel. "Hey, partner, you ready?" Tommy said to David.

"My friend Tommy and I have a double date," David said, as if Carlos should understand the priority.

Carlos put his head down and noticed that David's boots matched the ones on the steering wheel.

"Let's go, Danny!" Tommy said, impatiently.

"Danny?" Carlos asked.

"That's what they call me here in Miami," David said. "What's your address? I'll come over first thing tomorrow morning."

Tommy revved up the engine.

"I don't know it," Carlos said, unconvincingly. "I'll see you at school. You better hurry up. You don't want to make your friend wait."

David hopped in the convertible and the Chevy burned rubber away from Carlos.

CHAPTER XVI

David had to work hard to overcome having left his best friend standing alone after Carlos had so eagerly awaited their reunion. It had left a big wound, but their ten-year-old friendship survived it. Soon after, they again became inseparable, but only after David abandoned his friendship and short-lived association with Tommy.

Carlos and his mother lived in a clapboard cottage off a back alley. It was no bigger than a big dollhouse. Alicia had left for Belgium two weeks after their arrival in Miami. Her underground efforts on behalf of the Catholic Church at the University of Havana had paid off when the Catholic Church sent her abroad on a full scholarship.

Inside, the cottage was one small room plus a miniature bathroom. The one room had a hot plate, sink, an old icebox, a couch that turned into a bed where Carlos' mother slept, a small formica-top table with four rusted metal chairs, a standing lamp, a radio, and a black-and-white TV. Carlos slept on a rollaway bed pushed against a corner. The broom-size closet was ample since by the time Carlos and his mother left Cuba they were only allowed to leave with the clothes on their back.

The paint was peeling off the wall, the kitchen faucet leaked, the wall-heater blew cold air so they slept wearing most of the clothes they owned, and Carlos killed a minimum of seven cockroaches every day. But Mrs. Fernández always called it a bargain because it was less than a block from the bus stop, and she felt fortunate to afford their own place with the little money she made at the bookkeeper job she had found at a ladies' clothing store in downtown Miami.

◆━━◆━◆

One afternoon, a month after Carlos' arrival, Carlos and David anxiously rode their bicycles. David's first deed to regain Carlos' friendship had been to "buy" him a bicycle. Carlos was impressed with how much money David threw around, not knowing that David had obtained the bicycle the same way he had acquired his own—David stole it from a front yard not far from the school. During the entire two-hour ride to the address on the classified ad, David prayed for success in negotiating the price down to the three hundred dollars in his pockets—his entire fortune. Maybe it wasn't meant to be, he told himself, riding in silence next to Carlos.

It was love at first sight. It was a two-door, two-tone '55 Ford, baby blue body with dark blue top. David immediately knew it was meant to be his.

Imagining himself behind the wheel instantly helped rationalize his past deeds. He then hoped that, if he ended up forking out the entire three hundred dollars, the fuel tank would at least have enough gas to get him back to the camp. Carlos wouldn't be any financial help. He never had money. Fortunately, Carlos and his mother lived not far from the camp, so David wouldn't have to spend much gas on his best friend.

At thirty cents a gallon, David figured that with the help of a good tantalizing headline the next day, he would end up making enough money to afford to buy sufficient gas for the weekend dates he had already lined up.

The old lady who answered the door told them that she could not possibly sell her car for less than three hundred fifty dollars. First, David argued her down to three hundred and twenty dollars. Then, he negotiated the price down to three hundred ten. Finally, she dropped the price to three hundred in cash, plus mowing her lawn once a month for four months.

After David proved to the lady that he was sixteen by showing her his fake ID, he handed her all his money. The lady signed over the papers, and only then mentioned, as if an afterthought, something about a shimmy in the steering wheel. By that time, David was so anxious to get behind the wheel and so delighted that the car had a quarter tank of gas that he didn't pay attention to the seller's disclosure about the problem with the car's steering.

David and Carlos quickly stuffed their bikes into the trunk of the car and pulled the Ford out of the driveway. David floored it. Before they reached the end of the block, the car reached fifty miles an hour. The steering wheel suddenly went into a wild trembling fit. Panicked, David jumped on the brakes, smashing Carlos' head into the windshield. Luckily, Carlos had so much grease in his hair that his head slipped sideways when it hit the glass. It took them five minutes to clean enough of the gunk off the glass to be able to see out the windshield.

After learning at a gas station down the street that it would cost fifty bucks to get the steering problem fixed and finding out that the steering wheel only shook between fifty and fifty-five miles per hour, David concluded that the problem was no big deal.

After negotiating all week, David and Carlos reached an accord. David agreed to take Carlos along on double dates Friday nights, but only after Carlos promised to pay for the gas, plus a Coke and popcorn for both David and his date. Of course, David and his date would get the back seat when they reached the drive-in. This arrangement finally motivated Carlos to get a job delivering Western Union telegrams all day on Saturdays.

On the third Saturday of delivering telegrams, Carlos almost got arrested.

The night before, David had agreed to meet Carlos for lunch at the Burger King at the intersection of 27th Avenue and North West 95th Street. David had just finished waxing his car so when he pulled into the parking lot, he parked his baby in the shade. Without a hair out of place, he got out of his car and went inside the Burger King. Not finding Carlos, he took over the corner booth and looked out the window as he waited for Carlos.

A few minutes later, David saw Carlos ride his bicycle into the parking lot, sweating like a pig. At the same time, two young motorcycle cops left the Burger King sucking on milk shakes. Next to their Harley Davidson police motorcycles, the cops spotted Carlos chaining his bike to a light pole. Inside the Burger King, David cringed. He considered bailing out the back door, but instead he rushed toward Carlos and the cops.

"That your bike, kid?" the taller cop asked Carlos.

Carlos stood paralyzed, looking up at the two muscular cops towering over him, wearing black boots and big guns around their waists.

"What's the matter?" the more muscular cop said. "You deaf or something?"

"Yes," Carlos answered in his heavy Cuban accent. "It is my bicycle."

The two cops looked at each other. "I'll be damned," the taller cop said, "a blond, green-eyed spick."

Both cops cracked up at their own joke.

"I am from Cuba," Carlos said confused. "What is spick? Please."

The two cops almost peed in their pants laughing at Carlos.

David arrived and addressed the cops in perfect English. "Hi, can I help you with my friend here? He's just learning the language."

From Amigos to Friends

The two cops studied David and couldn't quite place him in the spick pigeonhole either. The taller one went to his motorcycle and pulled out a long list of numbers. He then went over to Carlos' bike and found a plate the size of a silver dollar attached to the bike's frame, right behind the seat. David saw the registration plate for the first time and the palms of his hands started sweating.

The cop matched the number on the plate to one on the list and he smiled. His partner smiled back.

David knew exactly what was going down. He gazed at his friend and realized Carlos, although he was oblivious to what was happening, was about to shit in his pants. David gave Carlos a look that said: 'Don't worry, everything is okay.'

"This here bike's been reported stolen," the muscular cop said.

"You said it was your bike, kid," the tall cop said to Carlos with an accusing tone, "so we're taking you in."

"In?" Carlos asked, filled with fear. He looked to David for help.

"Excuse me, officer," David said politely. "I gave my friend this bicycle for his twelfth birthday a week ago."

Carlos was about to protest that he was fifteen, not twelve, when David shut him up with a piercing dirty look.

David continued. "I bought it from another kid in the neighborhood for ten dollars."

"You really expect me to believe that?" the tall cop asked, skeptically.

"Yes, sir. It's the truth. His name is Tommy."

The muscular cop took a note pad and a pen out of a chest pocket and wrote the information down. "Where does he live? What's his address?"

"I don't know, sir," David continued. "I only know him from school."

"What's his last name?" the muscular cop asked.

"Jones. His name is Tommy Jones," David said right away.

The two cops went to the side and huddled. It was obvious that the tall cop wanted to haul both Carlos and David in, while the muscular one favored letting them go.

The tall one finally gave up, climbed on his Harley and, with an angry kick, cranked the engine back to life, and pulled out of the parking lot.

"Leave the bike chained there," the muscular cop said to Carlos, "and give me the keys. You two boys better get out of here quick before my buddy changes his mind and comes back looking for you."

Carlos gladly gave the keys to the cop and started heading in the direction of David's car. David diverted him and at a fast clip they took off walking down 27th Avenue.

When Carlos finally found his voice, he cursed David, telling him he couldn't wait to see Tommy beat the crap out of him for blaming Tommy for what David had done without even telling Carlos.

David informed Carlos that Tommy had skipped town two days ago, finding out that the cops were on his trail for breaking and entering all throughout northwest Miami for the past eighteen months. David didn't expect Tommy to return for the next few years.

David and Carlos went out dancing every Saturday night. Thirty miles north, in Fort Lauderdale, live bands rocked War Memorial Auditorium. The place was so big that they could always avoid last week's conquests and hit upon fresh material. Sure, there was competition, but the odds were certainly in their favor. The routine had a ninety percent track record. Carlos' good looks would melt the ice when approaching a new group of girls. Carlos would introduce his friend David, who was now close to six feet tall and packed one-hundred-and-seventy pounds of pure muscle. Carlos routinely tried to charge David for this service, but would always change his mind under the threat of bodily harm, plus the risk of having to walk back to Miami. To spice up the evening, Carlos and David had a standing one-dollar bet on who would get a new girl out of the dance and into the Ford, which was always strategically parked in the darkest part of the parking lot. The evening usually ended up in a tie, with David sweating it out and usually getting somebody to go out with him at the last minute. This was after Carlos had missed half the dance.

There was also a twenty-dollar bet on who would get lucky and get laid. It was a ton of money, but, after all, it would be a historic moment, since they were both virgins—a fact they vigorously denied to everyone else.

━━━━━

Sunday mornings were spent deep in the Everglades, training in guerrilla warfare to one day invade Cuba, again.

Crawling around a swamp full of mosquitos, snakes, and God-knows-what-else was no great way to get rid of Saturday night's hangover, but it was the only proven way to get out of attending Mass.

Not that sitting in an air-conditioned church was all that bad. It was the obligatory trip to confession that made risking one's life in the Everglades so appealing. It was one thing to spill your guts out to a priest who did not recognize you behind a confessional's screen and darkness, and quite another to confess your darkest thoughts and deeds to Father Michael while he chastised you by name.

The first and last time David went to confession was during his first week at camp. David stood in line until it was his turn to go into the confessional. He reluctantly entered the tiny space and kneeled down in almost total darkness.

"Forgive me, Father," David said in a low voice, attempting to disguise his identity, "for I have sinned."

"Good morning, David," Father Michael replied. "It sounds like you have a cold."

David was about to agree, but realizing that he would then have to turn around and confess the lie to Father Michael, he cleared his throat and returned his voice to normal. "I'm fine, Father Michael, thank you for your concern."

"So, how have you sinned, young man?"

David froze. Nothing would come out of his mouth.

"Come on, David." Father Michael said impatiently. "There are people waiting in line."

"I... ah... I've...," David tried, but the sins would just not come out of his mouth.

"How many people have you killed?"

"Killed?"

"Yeah, you know, shot, strangled, decapitated."

"I didn't do it. I haven't killed anyone. The worst thing I've done is play with myself... every night," David said in self-defense.

"Is that all?"

"And sometimes in the morning," David said, sheepishly.

"Son, if you don't give it a rest, it's going to fall off."

The embarrassment was life threatening, carving a deep wound in David's psyche. Never again!

When David learned that spending Sundays in the Everglades, training in guerrilla warfare to one day defeat the atheist Fidel Castro and recover the vast portfolio of Church-owned property in Cuba was a Church-endorsed alternative to Mass and confession, he immediately volunteered, becoming a rabid anti-Communist, freedom fighter.

Camouflaged deep in the swamps of the Everglades under an ancient cypress tree, David and Carlos wasted away the afternoon. "You think they're going to swallow the same 'we got lost' excuse again? We've already missed most of the afternoon drill," Carlos said, shooing flies away from his face.

"I hope so," David said. "I've accumulated so many mortal sins that I'd have to spend the rest of my life doing penance if we get kicked out and sent back to confession next Sunday."

"Stop bragging. The only thing they'll condemn to hell is your right hand."

David struck Carlos with an old broom David had been issued that Sunday to serve as a rifle.

"I still can't believe he's dead," Carlos said. "I think about Luis all the time."

David lowered his chin and shifted his eyes away from Carlos. David was surprised that Carlos had mentioned Luis. It was the first time that they had talked about their best friend. It had taken all this time for Carlos to be able to even say his name.

"You feel guilty, too, don't you?" Carlos said.

David shrugged his shoulders.

"It's not our fault that..."

David interrupted him, "If we had stayed..."

"It's not my fault!" Carlos cut him off. He was very firm about it, as if he had practiced saying it to convince himself.

"I didn't say that."

"It's not our fault that he killed himself," Carlos said firmly.

"Killed himself?"

"You don't think it was an accident?"

"Of course I do," David said.

"He'd jumped off that Bottle a hundred times."

"So what? He slipped."

"If you would've been around him the last month before it happened, you'd agree with me."

"I won't," David said. "That would only make it worse."

"It's not our fault. Luis wouldn't want us to feel that way. You know that."

"I wish he were here," David said.

They spent the rest of the afternoon swatting flies and trading stories about Luis, each trying to convince the other that he knew Luis better. In the end, they decided that given Luis' family situation, they were not to be blamed for whatever had happened.

Their conversation drifted away from Luis when Carlos mentioned that he missed his father much more than he had ever anticipated.

"I think I'm a lot like him," Carlos confessed. "Now that I've been away from him, he doesn't seem so bad."

"How about the fact that he stayed in Cuba with another woman?" David said, accusingly.

"I guess my parents stopped being in love with each other," Carlos said, shrugging his shoulders. "He must be happy with that woman. If he's in love with her, he should be with her, not with my mother."

"Don't you wish he was here with you?"

Carlos lowered his eyes. "I'm fifteen. I don't need him any more."

"You're full of shit, Carlos."

"Look at you. You're doing great without your father."

"You really think that?"

"You have a car."

"You don't realize how lucky you are to have your mother here. I didn't realize how much I needed my family until they didn't show up." David fell silent.

"They're going to get out," Carlos said, trying to improve David's mood. "It won't be long."

"I'm not counting on it. I'm alone and I'm prepared to make it on my own."

CHAPTER XVII

The first day of summer vacation of 1962 was hot—92 degrees in the shade and 98 percent humidity. David had no plans, nothing to do, nowhere to go. He had nobody to hang around with since Carlos and his mother had left the night before to visit relatives in New York for a whole month.

Summer school was out of the question. Sure, the school year had been a disaster, including two D's, one in chemistry and one in trigonometry. But, hey, going to summer school to repeat those classes and improve his grade point average as his counselor had recommended, was just plain overdoing it.

He was still living at the camp, one of only four kids left from the ones there when he arrived from Cuba. The others had been relocated to foster homes or Catholic boarding schools scattered throughout the United States. Everyday there were rumors about the camp closing down and everyone left being shipped out somewhere else.

In shorts and a T-shirt, David was scrubbing the white-wall tires of his car when Mr. Martínez appeared.

"You're going to Cleveland," Mr. Martínez announced. "The plane leaves at ten o'clock tomorrow morning." With nothing else to say, he simply turned around and walked away from David.

"I don't want to go to Cleveland," David said, chasing after Mr. Martínez. A knot formed in David's stomach and a chill cut deep down into his bones. This was the moment he had been expecting, but he was not handling it well.

"It has nothing to do with what you want," Martínez answered as he reached the front door. "Just make sure you leave the room clean before Father Michael comes to pick you up to take you to the airport." Martínez went in the house, leaving the front door wide open.

"Hey, Martínez, I'll miss you too," David yelled into the house.

Returning to his car, David suddenly realized that flying to Cleveland meant leaving his car behind. He rushed into the house and found Martínez in the kitchen, stuffing his face with a mango.

"I can't leave my car here. I'll drive it to Cleveland."

"You don't need it anymore. You're going to live and go to school in a walled-in seminary," Martínez said and then laughed so hard he covered David's T-shirt with mango spit.

"A seminary? Do I look like priest material to you?"

"The seminary has a boarding high school attached to it." Martínez stuffed the mango back in his mouth. "Very strict. No dating, no drinking. Who knows, you may get to like it."

"What about my car?"

"I'll give you fifty dollars for it. Or you can leave it out there on the street. It'll be stolen in a week."

An hour later, David found himself driving down the causeway, crossing the calm waters separating Miami from Miami Beach. He had all the windows down and the Beatles' "I Want to Hold Your Hand" blasting at full volume on WFUN. "Cleveland? Fucking Cleveland!" David swore as sailboats and motorboats traversed the sparkling blue waters on both sides of the causeway. Swollen cumulus clouds decorated a radiant sky. He didn't even know exactly where Cleveland was on the map, but he had never heard anything good about it either.

From Amigos to Friends

Reaching South Beach, he found a free parking space on Collins and 12th. He stripped down to his bathing suit and locked his T-shirt, pants, and sneakers in the trunk of his car. He headed down to the water. The hot sand felt good between his toes. He reached the surf and faced south toward Cuba. For the first time in months, he wished he could swim back to his homeland. He felt alone, sad, empty of all hope. Cleveland! Why me? Why not New York or California? Fucking Cleveland! He shook his head and with the surf lapping his feet he headed north. A seminary! A fucking seminary!

Lost in his own despair, David drifted past the public beach and entered the private beach area in front of the hotels starting on 15th Avenue. Suddenly, a piercing scream brought him back from Cleveland. He spotted a woman screaming hysterically with the water up to her chin thirty yards out. A toddler about his brother's age, wearing a Donald Duck life-saver, was drifting away from her, pulled out to sea by the undertow. David ran into the ocean and swam after the kid. He swam as fast as he could, popping his head out of the water from time to time to make sure he was headed in the right direction. He could hear different voices yelling for help. The kid kept drifting out to sea. David thought of his brother and tapped into an unknown reservoir of energy and swam faster. He passed the kid's mother. "I can't swim," she said, sobbing hysterically, as if apologizing for her lack of action. Her pain made David swim even faster. He was gaining on the kid, who was now thrashing about in a panic. David's legs began to cramp up. When David was about ten yards from the child, he saw the boy tip over his lifesaver and disappear underwater. David took a deep breath and dove underwater, ignoring all concerns about risking his own life, imagining that he was saving his own brother. The water was clear enough that he spotted the kid sinking toward the bottom. Without reaching for air, David dove down another ten feet underwater and grabbed the boy by his tiny wrist. Seconds later, they both broke the surface, coughing and gasping for breath. The crowd that had gathered back on the beach went wild. Exhausted and worried because both his legs kept cramping up, David tried to calm the boy down. The boy, driven by his instinct for survival, kept hitting and kicking David. The undertow kept taking them further out to sea. David realized he might have to let the kid drown if he was to have any chance of surviving himself.

"Help me, help me," the boy said as if reading David's mind.

"I will," David promised him, "but you have to trust me and stop fighting me. Just relax and try to float. You know how to float on your back?"

The boy did, and spotting the lifesaver, they reached it. David was able to get the boy back in the lifesaver.

Together they floated out to sea until a boat picked them up. David returned with the child to a hero's welcome back at the beach. All the teenaged girls asked David for a date. The boy's mother, a tall blonde in her late twenties, gave David an intense hug. Several middle-aged hotel guests stuffed dollar bills in his hands. The hotel manager offered David a cash reward, without specifying how much. Instead, David asked the manager if he could have a job for the summer. "He'll make a great lifeguard," several people in the crowd suggested to the manager. On the spot, the manager fired the lifeguard for failing to do his job and gave it to David. David told the manager that he had just arrived from Cleveland and had no place to stay. The manager gratefully threw in room and board.

"It was a bargain," the manager was heard bragging later at a staff meeting. "Do you know how much it would have cost the hotel had that kid drowned? The bad publicity alone would have cost me my job."

The room wasn't much. It was a half basement at the very bottom of the hotel. Its tiny closet was ample, since David had decided not to go back to the camp and chance ending up in Cleveland. He was on top of the world. He had everything. One T-shirt, a pair of pants, sneakers, a bathing suit, a fist full of dollars, a full-time job as a lifeguard in a hotel in Miami Beach, room and board, and his Ford. What else would a fifteen-year-old possibly want out of life?

That same night in his new room at the hotel, David was awakened in the middle of the night from a deep sleep by a soft, persistent knock on the door. He cracked the door open and peeked out into the hallway. To his surprise, he found the kid's mother standing in front of him.

"I'm here to thank you for saving my son," she said as she slipped inside his room.

That night David lost his virginity.

David looked for her the next day, but to his disappointment, he found out she and her son had checked out early that morning.

The transient nature of the hotel had its advantages in that every day was a new adventure, never knowing from day to day what gorgeous female would show up at the swimming pool.

The days were long. The job included not only keeping an eye out on the pool and the ocean to make sure not to get fired if somebody else saved a guest from drowning when you were distracted, but also greeting the guests as they arrived by the pool, verifying that they were registered guests of the hotel, and assigning them lounge chairs and issuing towels.

Two weeks after moving into the hotel, since leaving the camp unannounced to escape ending up in Cleveland, David wrote his parents in Cuba. In the letter he rationalized his actions by inventing a sorry story about finding out that the school in Cleveland was really a reform school. Not convinced that it helped vindicate him after reading the letter several times, he rewrote the letter, changing the reform school to a school for mentally retarded teenagers. And not wanting to jeopardize a very promising summer by telling his parents where he was staying, he told them he had found a good-paying construction job for the summer. He told them he was living with some friends he did not identify, and he asked them to write to him at Carlos' address.

The first three weeks at the hotel flew by so quickly that he hardly missed Carlos. The only times David thought of him was when planning how to most dramatically spring on Carlos that David was no longer a virgin and that Carlos owed him twenty bucks. David had prepared himself, knowing that Carlos would return with some lame story about getting laid in New York. Using his fresh experience and insight into the subject of sex, David had woven an elaborate list of interrogation questions to force Carlos to admit that he was still a virgin.

CHAPTER XVIII

Poolside on a cloudy afternoon, David was working his newfound charm on a gorgeous seventeen-year-old blonde beauty that had checked into the hotel with her parents that afternoon. Suddenly, from out of the corner of his eye, David spotted a spectacular-looking older woman, poured into a provocative bikini. He guessed that she was in her mid-twenties.

David excused himself, pointing out that he needed to go help this new hotel guest, and with great expectations he rushed to find out who this incredible looking woman was.

"Hi, I'm David... your lifeguard. Can I get a lounge chair for you?" he said, trying hard not to stare at her lovely figure that was barely covered by her very skimpy bikini. "And if you decide to drown, I'm the lucky one who gets to rescue you." That line always works. A great icebreaker, he thought.

She cracked a smile and checked him up and down. "Sugar, you make drowning an appealing proposition," she said in a slow, Southern drawl that covered David's skin with goose bumps. "Honey, get me a good spot in the sun so I can get a tan as yummy as yours."

After strategically parking her so that he could command a perfect view of her super body, David went to the house phone and dialed the front desk. "This is David by the pool. I need to verify a hotel guest. Last name is Smith... first name Amanda... room 306. By the way, is she alone...or is she part of a larger group?" This was David's way to discreetly find out if a male was attached.

"There's a Mr. and Mrs. Goldberg in 306," said the front desk clerk.

"You sure about that?"

"Actually, there's no Smith registered at the hotel," the clerk said. "You better ask her to leave, you know the rules."

David hung up. Ask her to leave? Are you kidding? Are you crazy? I want her here the rest of the summer, David thought as he went directly to her.

As David opened his mouth, she handed him a bottle of Coppertone. "Sugar, would you do the back of my legs?" She lay flat on her stomach and undid her bikini top.

David sat at the edge of her lounge chair and with precision, to make sure he didn't miss a spot, and doing everything possible to prolong the pleasure of stroking her long, firm legs, David complied. "There seems to be a mistake," he said casually. "There's no one by the name of Amanda Smith in room 306, or in any other room. Do you go by any other name?"

She slowly sat up on the lounge chair next to David and barely kept herself inside the bikini as she strapped the top back on. "I've been found out. Guilty as all sin," she said with a mischievous grin. "So what happens now, Sugar? You throw me out into the ocean? It's too bad. I was enjoying so much getting to know each other so intimately."

"You can stay. It's almost closing time," he said like a big shot doing her some kind of huge favor. "You doing anything tonight?"

"I'm a working girl, Honey," she said in that sweet as pie Southern drawl that has served women from the South so well for centuries.

"Where do you work?"

"I'm a cocktail waitress, Honey," she said, collecting all her things in a beach bag.

From Amigos to Friends

"I don't mind waiting up late. Where do you want to meet?"

"Let's make it simple. I'll come to your place at eleven thirty tonight and let's see if I can talk you into letting me use the pool everyday. Where do you live, Hon?"

At midnight that night, David paced his small room. He had canceled all his plans for the night, taken a long nap, done some chin-ups and pushups, eaten a big steak dinner with two glasses of milk to build up his stamina, and had tried to make his semi-basement room as presentable as possible. The biggest improvement was taking his dirty clothes to the laundry. The room smelled a lot better after that.

At quarter past midnight, there was a knock on the door. David took a deep breath and went to answer the door. Without a word, Amanda strolled into the room, wearing a scorching outfit. She sat on the edge of the bed and pulled a six-pack of beer out of a grocery bag she brought with her.

All David could do was control himself from drooling all over the new shirt he was wearing.

Amanda popped open a can of beer and with gusto took a long swallow.

David stared at her long shapely legs and low cut top.

She popped open another can of beer and offered it to David.

He wanted no part of it. He hated how it tasted and the one time he had been intimidated by his camp-mates to drink a couple of beers at the beach, he had ended up throwing up underwater so no one could tell.

"Come over here and have a beer with me, Sugar," Amanda said, still sitting at the edge of his bed.

As fast as you could say no thanks, David was by her side drinking out of the cold beer can Amanda handed him.

Pelayo "Pete" Garcia

Two hours later, as Amanda left his room, David concluded that short of spending the rest of his life in jail, he would let Amanda use the hotel's pool and sauna everyday. Worst case, he'd end up in Cleveland. It was definitely worth the risk, he decided. The room suddenly started spinning out of control. David crawled out of bed past the empty beer cans on the floor, weaved to the bathroom, hung on to the sides of the toilet bowl, and completely drunk, puked his guts out.

But the next day he wasn't so sure that his judgment had been as clear as it should've been and that promising Amanda the use of the hotel facilities had been such a good idea.

She arrived at midday. It was a perfect summer day and the pool was crowded with an assortment of couples and families, a noisy crowd enjoying themselves. The only way to describe what happened is to say that she stopped the place cold. The closest thing to it had occurred a week earlier when out of nowhere a lightning bolt had struck near the pool, paralyzing everyone in mid-sentence. The loud clicking of her high heels against the concrete deck interrupted every conversation. And her micro, skin-tone bikini made the blood of every male rush down to their shorts, and made every woman fire dirty, accusatory looks at their male companions.

David tried to park her in a back corner of the pool deck, but she objected loud enough to motivate David to agree to move her front and center as she demanded.

Panicked, David realized the agreement was not going to work out. He took her to the side and pleaded with her to void the deal. "No way," she said. "You already collected your side of the bargain, Pal."

So, things had quickly deteriorated from Sugar to Pal, all within the first ten minutes—not a good sign, David concluded.

From Amigos to Friends

"I'll tell the hotel manager you lured me last night into your room in his hotel," she threatened him, convincingly enough to prompt David to back off.

◆━◆━◆

From then on, their nights together were not much different from the first, except that David became able to drink more and more beer before passing out drunk in his bed.

One particular night, Amanda arrived very late to his room, acting very silly, very drunk. She reached in the paper sack she brought with her and out came a Coca Cola bottle and a bottle of rum. "Hand me a couple of glasses, would you, Sugar?"

Minutes later, she handed David a glass. "Here, try this, Sugar. I'm sure you'll like it. They call it Cuba Libre." She laughed her head off with the alcohol helping her believe she had just said the funniest thing in the world.

David hesitated. He wanted to party with her, but he had never had hard liquor.

Amanda finished her drink and mixed herself another full glass. She started laughing, as if she had just heard something hilarious. "Try it. You'll like it."

"I don't want any. Why didn't you bring us some beer?" He said and tried to kiss her.

She puckered her lips and said, " No drinky, no kissy, big boy."

After the third rum and Coke, David couldn't stop laughing, at nothing in particular. A huge grin plastered on his face.

"I told you you'd like it," Amanda said, jumping up and down on the bed. The bed suddenly collapsed with a thunderous crash. Amanda and David jumped out of bed and rolled around on the floor in side-splitting fits of laughter. Then David heard a firm banging on the door. He tried to get serious before he answered it. He opened the door a crack and found the hotel security guard staring back at him.

"Sorry about the noise, George," David said, trying to act serious.

The guard tried to look inside David's room.

"Just a little party. I'll send everybody home in a few minutes."

"Keep the noise down, amigo," the security guard said and David closed the door in his face.

David turned around and found himself facing the barrel of a snub-nose .32 revolver. "Keep the noise down, amigo," Amanda said, imitating the security guard's voice. She cocked the hammer back and embedded the cold barrel against his forehead, instantly sobering David right up. She then went off in a fit of laughter.

David grabbed the gun away from her and very carefully brought the hammer back down in place. He checked, and, sure enough, the gun was fully loaded.

"Are you crazy! You could've killed me! Time for you to go home!"

She layed on the bed and struck a very sexy pose. "You sure you're done for the night, Sugar?" She slithered around the half-collapsed bed and her pose turned from sexy to provocative.

David carefully put the gun down on the one chair in the room and jumped in bed with her. She avoided him and getting out of bed proceeded to mix them a couple more rum and Cokes.

When she drank hers and didn't give him his glass, David got mad and started chasing her all around the room. She tried to drink his drink all by herself, giggling the whole time.

"You can't get me! You can't get me!" she chanted.

"Bad girl! Amanda... you're a bad girl!"

"You can't get me! You can't get me!" she continued tauntingly.

"I'm going to spank you when I catch you. Amanda's a bad girl. I'm going to spank her!"

From Amigos to Friends

She jumped onto the bed and David jumped in after her. The bed finally collapsed completely, this time with one great big bang.

He wrestled the glass of rum and Coke away from her and gulped down as much of it as he could, while at the same time fighting off her efforts to get to his drink.

David barely heard the loud banging at the door. He reluctantly dragged himself off the mattress, now on the floor, and answered the door. It was George, the security guard.

CHAPTER XIX

David escaped any negative consequences from his Rum-driven night with Amanda by convincing George that David would get him a couple of bottles of Bacardi Rum, counting on Amanda to steal them from the bar where she worked and where she stole all the booze they drank all the time.

Carlos was back in town by then, so David phoned him and without giving his best friend any details, he arranged to have Carlos meet him late that afternoon at the hotel. That same night, David had a date with Amanda. As always, preparing for Carlos' return took a lot of planning, given all the ammunition David had at his disposal. He strongly suspected that after four weeks apart, Carlos had also prepared for their reunion and would show up full of exaggerations, half-truths, and outright lies, all in an immature effort to achieve exactly the same goal that David had in mind. David told Carlos just enough to get him to show up at the hotel, but he skipped any mention about working at the hotel, or living there. "Just go to the front desk and ask if I've arrived. I'll see you there at five o'clock in the afternoon," David had said.

Punctual as ever, Carlos arrived at the hotel pool at six minutes after five—exactly the time it had taken Carlos to find out from the front desk that David was the hotel's lifeguard and a hero for having saved a kid's life at the risk of his own. David had made the front desk clerk memorize exactly how to give Carlos this information. Five o'clock was the perfect time of the day. By then no one would be arriving at the pool wanting a lounge chair and towels, diminishing the image of a true lifeguard. He had paid George, the security guard, five bucks to pick up the towels and close the pool down at the end of the day. And then for the climax to this exquisite plan to torture Carlos' ego—Amanda would show up. David would simply excuse himself and send Carlos home after explaining he had a hot date with Amanda.

Looking muscular and tanned, perched on the lifeguard stand, gazing out to the horizon with an intense, alert eye out for swimmers in distress, David acted irritated when three feet underneath him, Carlos called out his name. David slid his sunglasses down the bridge of his nose and said, "Carlos, man, you need to get some sun. You look so pale. Are you sick?"

"You owe me twenty bucks," Carlos said, failing miserably to disguise his realization that he was outgunned.

David basked in the glory of knowing that this ambush ranked up there with the time when he and Luis had broadsided Carlos with the motorcycles and the motorcycle club. David jumped down from his pedestal and they hugged. "If you're lucky and you're not lying like you always do, we're even," David said, stretching out on a lounge chair overlooking the ocean. "I'm having one incredible summer. You can imagine, being a lifeguard and all." David could tell from Carlos' shifty eyes that he was probably still a virgin, but he wasn't quite sure.

"I had a great time in New York. Miami is a farm town in comparison. The minute I get out of high school I'm out of here," Carlos said, trying to act sophisticated. "The women in New York. Notice that I said women, not girls, real women who are into sex."

"So, Carlos, how many times did you do it?"

"Three times," Carlos responded immediately.

Just as David had expected, Carlos had come well prepared.

"Three different girls, I mean women, or three times with the same one?"

"That's right, three different ones," Carlos said with pride.

"No repeats, I see," David said. "You must be pretty bad when they don't come back for more."

David's comment shook Carlos up. "No, I'm the one who decided not to repeat," Carlos rallied back. "Are you kidding me, they were throwing themselves at my feet."

David had one final bullet to pierce through Carlos' pack of lies. It was going to be a big sacrifice for David, but in the long run it would be a lifelong debt that Carlos would owe him. "It's too bad that you're not still a virgin," David said, setting out the hook and bait.

"What do you mean?" Carlos asked, suspiciously.

"Forget it. It doesn't matter now."

"Tell me anyway. What the hell."

"What you mean is that you're still a virgin, right?" David pressed on.

"Give me a break, okay? I told you, three times. With three different women."

"That's too bad. You see, I had a surprise for you. But only if you'd come back still a virgin."

"What kind of surprise?"

"This woman that I've been seeing. She's really hot. I've told her about you. She has this thing for virgins. I was going to introduce you to her tonight. But, you're not a virgin anymore."

"I've only done it three times. That's almost a virgin."

"No, you're either a virgin, or you're not."

"That doesn't make any sense," Carlos complained. "Wait a minute, just tell her I'm a virgin. She can't tell."

"I can't do that. She's a good friend. I don't know about you, but I don't lie to my friends," David said. "You wouldn't lie to me, right?"

"I'll lie to her. She's not my friend."

"Sorry, she'll ask me and I'll have to tell her you've been with three girls, excuse me, three women."

At dusk, Amanda appeared in the distance, and Carlos' eyes almost popped out of his head. "Hi, David," she called out and headed in their direction.

"Is that her?" Carlos asked, breaking into a sweat.

"There she is. It's too bad you're not a virgin anymore. She's incredible."

"Come on, David. Let's lie to her. We've been friends since kindergarten. How long have you known her? Two weeks?"

"It wouldn't do any good. I don't know how, but she can tell. If you're not a virgin she'll be able to tell right away. It's spooky. It's like she's psychic, or something."

Amanda was almost by their side when Carlos finally broke down. "David, I'm still a virgin, I swear. You'll see. She'll tell you it's true. I want her."

Amanda arrived by their side with enough sensuality to rise a dead man from his grave. Up and down, she checked Carlos out. Carlos was speechless. "Hi, Sugar," she said to David while flirting with Carlos. "Who's the cute blond?"

"Amanda, meet my best friend Carlos," David said. "As you can see, he's a virgin. I know you're going to be disappointed at not being with me, but I'd like for you to go out with Carlos tonight." David flipped his room key to Amanda. She caught the key in midair.

◆━◆━◆

Carlos turned bright red. Amanda thought about it for no more than a split second. "My pleasure," she said, taking Carlos' hand.

For the rest of the summer, for two dollars a day, twenty-five percent of the tips plus all the dates he could round up, David subcontracted to Carlos the job of assigning lounge chairs, handing out towels, and cleaning up the pool area at the end of the day.

David called it a win-win situation.

Carlos wasn't making much money, because between spending two dollars a day for bus fare to and from his mother's house and buying lunch to avoid all the cracks about bringing a brown bag lunch from home, he was basically breaking even. He was in this deal for the girls. It made getting up at five o'clock in the morning to take three different buses to get to the hotel well worth it.

Carlos would have tried to convince his mother to let him spend the night with David at the hotel, but he was not able to tell his mother where David was staying. David feared that Mrs. Fernández would immediately write his parents, who would promptly arrange to have him shipped off to Cleveland. So Carlos endured the two-hour commute each way, every day. The thought of turning David in and ending up with the lifeguard job himself only occurred to Carlos three or four times a day.

Carlos felt bad for his mother. Life was hard for her as an exile. Mr. Fernández had stayed behind in Cuba and hardly ever returned her weekly letters. Her daughter had married and had decided to stay in Belgium permanently. Mrs. Fernández now worked as a seamstress in a clothing factory. It was backbreaking piecework, rushing through zipper after zipper to make enough money to afford to move into a two-bedroom apartment, and to provide three meals a day and some decent clothes for her son.

David never looked back on the deal. He enjoyed having Carlos to boss around, and having gotten rid of the menial part of the job, he concentrated on showing off his lifeguard status, reaping all the attention and benefits of being center stage. As always, Carlos' good looks made him tough competition, but having to catch a bus back to his mother's house by eight o'clock at night made Carlos a much weaker competitor. After all, David had his own room in the hotel.

David had kept his whereabouts concealed from his parents. He wrote to them, and at Carlos' house David received loving letters from his mother, pleading for him to surface, and blistering ultimatums from his father to return to the camp. By now, he had decided that he had a good thing going at the hotel, and going back to high school was nothing but a big waste of time.

In early September, a powerful hurricane brewing off the coast of Nassau and dead reckoning toward Miami Beach practically emptied the hotel. Following an announcement by the National Hurricane Center warning that the hurricane's eye would strike South Beach that night, the hotel manager instructed David and Carlos to close the pool down immediately and to store all poolside furniture and equipment in the hotel's basement. The hotel became a beehive of activity: guests checking out as fast as taxis could be fetched, employees running around with rolls of masking tape, reinforcing all the windows, and Carlos and David running down the beach chasing after runaway beach umbrellas.

Carlos initially worried about leaving his mother alone during a hurricane, when David suggested turning the natural disaster into an opportunity for Carlos to spend the night. "We're having a hurricane party," David reminded him.

"I don't know. My mother is going to be very mad at me if I don't go home," Carlos said, ringing his hands. "I'm worried that she won't be safe by herself."

"Hurricanes are overrated. It's just a little rain and wind," David said as the sky threatened to empty and he tried to hold onto a lounge chair ready to fly off to Kansas. "It's too late now anyway. I'm sure the buses have stopped running."

"That's a good point," Carlos said. "It's not my fault I have to stay."

"Exactly. Get on the phone and tell her you're stranded here," David said. "Make sure you don't mention my name."

Carlos thought of his mother dying alone, calling out his name. He bolted for the lobby. "I'm going home. I can't leave my mother all alone."

Carlos ran into Amanda as she stepped out of the lobby into the torrential rain. She was carrying a grocery bag in each arm. "Hi, Sugar, where you going in such a rush?" she asked, getting soaked. "I hope you're staying for the hurricane party."

"Are you going to be there?" Carlos asked with a thin line of drool marking his lower jaw.

"Me and four of my best-looking girlfriends. I'm so excited. Look at all the booze I brought," Amanda said, showing Carlos the two shopping bags full of hard liquor.

"Of course I'm going to the party," Carlos said. "Here, let me help you with those bags."

David convinced the hotel manager that his room in the basement would flood and that since the hotel was practically empty, it would be safer if he spent the hurricane in one of the penthouse suites. That way David would keep an eye out for hurricane damages.

The word about David hosting a hurricane party in a penthouse suite of the hotel with plenty of booze spread like wildfire around the underbelly of South Beach.

Before the eye of the hurricane arrived at ten minutes before midnight, the suite had standing room only. A few guests were fully clothed, but most were down to their bathing suits. Carlos had the bright idea of leaving a window open to make sure to notice the end of the howling winds and pouring rain, marking the few minutes of complete calm as the eye of the hurricane passed by. When the rain stopped pouring in through the window, the room emptied with a stampede, as party animals headed down to the ocean to swim until the second half of the hurricane arrived. Fortunately for David, the lights had gone out in the building, and he hoped as he headed down the hallway that the hotel manager would not discover his entourage, running through the hotel.

The fun came to a sudden halt when David's companions—soaking wet on their way back to the party from their dip in the ocean—were spotted by the hotel manager when the building lights suddenly returned. The group dispersed in different directions, trying to avoid being thrown out of the hotel now that the hurricane had returned in full force.

David bolted up the stairs and reached the suite. He quickly climbed into someone's pair of pants and with Carlos' help, he threw out the open window all the bottles of booze they could find—not an easy task with the wind howling at over one hundred miles per hour. The hotel manager stepped over Amanda who had passed out in front of the door to the suite. He took one look inside the room and stomped back to the lobby. The party ended with Carlos and David chasing everyone out of the room, warning them to get out of the hotel, hurricane or no hurricane, before the police arrived.

After cleaning the suite of any incriminating evidence, David and Carlos dragged Amanda back down into David's room in the basement. Exhausted and pacified by all the alcohol, they both passed out on either side of her.

When they woke up the next morning, Amanda was gone. She must have left in a hurry, because she had left behind her bra in the middle of the room, a ton of makeup in the bathroom, and her .38 caliber revolver was left on the chair. The gun had probably dropped out of her purse.

Carlos hurried back to his mother's house, worried about her safety and blaming and cursing David for "forcing" him to stay.

David hid Amanda's revolver under his mattress, stashed all the bottles of booze in the closet, and then went out to the pool to survey the damage. Except for a few broken shutters, the place had held up well. The tide was way up and the surf pounded the hotel's seawall. The wind howled and pulled on the palm trees scattered around the pool deck. But the rain had stopped.

Within ten minutes, the hotel manager appeared and said, "You're fired." Those words meant being out on the street with less than fifty bucks to his name and without much chance of finding another job in the area, not without a recommendation. Maybe he could scout the beach for another save-a-kid-from-drowning hero opportunity.

David returned to his room resolved to gather his few possessions, hop in his Ford, and once at an intersection he would flip a coin to decide which direction to go.

He heard a knock on the door and hoped it would be Amanda, returning to get her gun. He was ready to leave and didn't know what to do with the .38 still under the mattress. He hoped that she would have forgotten about the booze so that he could keep it all for himself.

He answered the door ready to plant a big kiss on Amanda's delicious lips. Instead, he found two huge suits with crew cuts crowding the hallway. The older one flashed a badge in front of David's face. "Miami Beach police detectives." With that they let themselves in the room. "Are you David Oviedo?"

The gun! David immediately thought of the gun and sat down at the edge of the bed, right over the gun. "That's my name. I'm the lifeguard of the hotel." The booze! David remembered and prayed that the detectives would stay away from the closet.

"Ex-lifeguard," the other one said. "We understand you had one hell of a wild party here last night."

"Maybe it got a little out of hand. You know, hurricane parties and all. Actually, it was up on the sixth floor," David said and slowly moved toward the door. "I'll take you up there."

The older one shoved David back on the bed. "Sit down, kid."

David panicked, noticing that the other detective was starting to rummage through the room. That moment David made the most daring decision of his young life. "I want to tell you right away that I'm Cuban and a member of an underground guerrilla group that will be invading Cuba in the very near future."

The detectives posted themselves in front of David, trying to figure out his angle.

"I want to come clean and show you the weapon I've been trained with to assassinate Fidel Castro." David stood and reached under the mattress.

Both detectives drew their weapons. "Freeze, kid."

David moved aside and one of the suits yanked the mattress off the frame. Amanda's .38 looked puny. "That? You're going to kill Castro with that?" Both suits cracked up, returning their guns to their holsters. "Shit, boy, I thought you said you had a weapon. That's a girl's gun."

David wanted to tell them how right they were. "It'll do the job. I just have to get close enough to him."

David then dropped a few CIA names belonging to the group that had tried to train him and Carlos in the Everglades on Sunday afternoons. The detectives, both rabidly anti-Communist and anxious to see Castro dead so all the "spicks" would go back to Cuba, didn't believe a word David said, but decided to leave David behind just in case there was some truth to it. They did take the gun with them, knowing that the "spicks" had plenty of guns hidden in the Everglades.

David rushed to the door and made sure it was properly locked. He then returned to the bed and collapsed, taking deep breaths to calm himself down. He prayed out loud every prayer he could remember, giving thanks for not having been hauled away to jail. Suddenly, he had a major case of paranoia, visualizing the detectives rushing back to his room, gun in hand, after sitting in their car in the parking lot realizing that David's story about the assassination of Castro was at best preposterous, or after calling on the police car radio the gun's serial number and finding out that gun was wanted for a rash of hideous murders. David jumped out of bed and went to work: he emptied in the toilet the bottles of booze. Twelve times he flushed the toilet, while crossing himself to chase evil spirits away. Finished, he stuffed all his belongings in a dirty pillowcase, and he bolted out of the room.

Out in the hallway, he realized he had no plan, nowhere to go. He went out to the water's edge and headed South. He walked and thought for hours, sweating, thinking of what would have happened if he hadn't lucked out and bullshitted his way out of it.

I can't even imagine my parents back in Cuba finding out that I was almost thrown in jail for the illegal possession of a firearm. They would never swallow the story about me as a potential assassin of Fidel Castro. They would kill me. Of course they would never get to, considering the lengthy jail sentence I would serve. I'd be the one doing the punishment. Devastating emotional punishment. I can just hear my mother's favorite saying: David, everything you do is a reflection of your mother and father.

By dusk, his feet were covered with blisters, and, exhausted, he sat down on the sand gazing south toward Cuba. It then flashed through his mind that having a son with a criminal record would surely deny his parents and brother the right to enter the United States, or any other country in the world, condemning them to live and suffer in Cuba for the rest of their lives. And all because David had turned into a selfish, petty hedonist.

He assumed that once let out of jail after spending his youth in a maximum security prison, he would be deported back to Cuba, and he would have to endure the shame of having soiled his family's honor. My parents would have no sympathy for me. My father always said that I must accept responsibility for my own actions. He would never, ever speak to me again. I would be ruining their lives, especially my brother's life. My crimes would be the cause of my brother enduring a lost life. An empty life devoid of opportunities to achieve his potential, to become who he chose to become as my parents explained to me at that fancy restaurant in Havana the night they told me I would leave for Miami.

David spent the night by the water's edge, realizing, over and over, how close he had come to permanently ruining his life. He finally confronted what he had known all along, that he had mishandled everything since he had arrived in Miami. He was embarrassed with himself. He had promised his parents that he would handle himself in a way that they would be proud. Instead, he had cast aside everything his parents had taught him and had broken his promise to them, as well as their trust in him.

A spectacular sunrise marked the first day of the rest of his life, as his mother had told him every day as she awoke him. David closed his eyes and made a sacred vow with himself to change his ways, to become the honest, principled man that he wanted to be and his parents expected him to become. From that moment on he didn't need anyone's supervision to make sure his actions were that of a gentleman.

Back at the hotel's parking lot, he reached his Ford parked out on the lot. He knew where he wanted to go. He had thought about it before. Now that he had taken his vow, he was ready.

David reached Carlos' house and knocked on the front door.

Carlos, in his pajamas and with sleep in his eyes, answered the door. "You look like shit," Carlos said. "What happened..."

David interrupted Carlos. "What do you think about asking your mother if I can live with you guys... until we graduate from high school?" David said. "I would really like to do that."

"High school? I thought we were going to skip it. That's boring, man. We have better things to do."

"We're full of shit, you know that? We're lucky as hell we haven't messed up our lives already." David said. "We act tough, but all we are is a couple of punks."

"I've decided to move out of my mother's house," Carlos said like a big shot. "It'll be hard on her, but I have to think about myself now. She'll survive it."

"You're a jerk, Carlos."

"Besides, I know you: In a week you'll change your mind and take off in your car."

David took out his wallet and found his fake driver's license. He showed it to Carlos and then ripped it in half. Carlos tried to stop him, but David proceeded to rip the fake driver's license into little pieces. Carlos couldn't believe his eyes. He tried to protest, but the words wouldn't come out.

"We're parking the Ford in your driveway for the next four months," David said, "until I'm sixteen, and I can get a legal driver's license."

"You're nuts. How are we going to get to the dances in Fort Lauderdale? How about all the dates I've lined up?"

David shrugged his shoulders.

They stood in silence.

"I don't know what my mother will say," Carlos mumbled. "We're really broke."

"I'll pay my way. I'll go back to selling newspapers out on the streets if I have to."

"It's okay with me, but I don't know. We can ask her."

"Good, good," David said.

"Let's think of some really good reason so that she can't say no," Carlos said.

"How about if we tell her that last night during the hurricane I saved your life?" David suggested.

"You? Saved my life?" Carlos said, his voice raising. "She'd never fall for that."

"Oh, you don't think it's possible?"

"Of course not!"

"You're always needing my help," David said. "It's been that way since I can remember."

"You're full of it," Carlos said.

"Oh, yeah, and who got you laid for the first time?"

"That's different. Besides, it wasn't my first time."

"You're full of shit, Carlos!"

"You are!"

"You..." David studied Carlos, then looked away—off into the morning sun. Finally, he turned back to his best friend, nodding slightly. "You're right, Carlos. I'm full of it. But... I'm working on it."

EPILOGUE

"Dad! Dad! Wake up!"

I heard a voice calling, my shoulder being shaken.

"Come on, Dad! Wake up!"

I opened my eyes and found myself slouched on the chair in my son's room. My back was killing me, as if a hot poker was burning through to my spine.

"Dad, we overslept!" my eleven-year-old son Danny said in a panic.

A severe headache kicked in with a vengeance.

"Get up! Hurry up!"

I didn't have a clue about what he was talking about. I couldn't even remember what day it was.

"Dad, come on, hurry up!"

Not wanting to tarnish my infallible parental image, I hedged my bets. "What time is it?"

Danny pulled hard on my arm, trying to get me out of the chair.

"If you hurry, we'll still make it on time!" he said.

"Is your mom up yet?" I asked, fishing for clues.

Suddenly, spotting the bowl with a single grape and seeds, it all came rushing back into focus.

We ran out of the house.

I pushed the old '55 Ford hard. I'd restored the exterior and interior, but the engine had a ways to go.

Luckily, the plane was late arriving in San Diego, something about all planes originating in New York being delayed because of a snowstorm on the east coast.

We ran to the gate just in time to see them coming down the jet way.

Carlos and Luis had not changed much since our yearly reunion last January.

When both of our wives became pregnant with boys at about the same time, Carlos and I realized that both of us couldn't name our sons after our best friend Luis. There was no disagreement whatsoever about that.

The conflict was over who would get to do so. After extensive long-distance phone negotiations between San Diego and New York, we were hopelessly deadlocked.

In the end, Carlos won the toss and ended up naming his kid Luis.

THE END